A Notion of Pelicans

A Notion of Pelicans

To Jan and John,
who share important
traits with me ...
  Finns + art ...

by

Donna Salli

♡

Donna Salli

NORTH STAR PRESS OF ST. CLOUD, INC.
St. Cloud, Minnesota

First edition: September 2016

Printed in the United States of America.

Published by
North Star Press of St. Cloud, Inc.
P.O. Box 451
St. Cloud, MN 56302

northstarpress.com

For Bruce

"Tell all the Truth but tell it slant—"
- Emily Dickinson

Contents

Pelican Church: The "Family"

"Blest be the tie that binds..."
John Fawcett, Hymnodist, 1782

Lavinia Hoope Hansen = Henry Hansen
"The Founding Mother"   *"Lavinia's Helpmate"*
1848-1932

Pastor Jack Grange, Retired
"The Perfect Father"

Pastor Richard Cross = Serena Cross
"The Father"   *"The Father's Wife"*
❖ **Andy, Scott & Chelsey Cross**
"Everyone's Kids"

Antonia Sprague-Heller ≈ Sam Heller
"The Odd Sister"   *"The Lost Son"*

Claire Collier ÷ Paul Collier
"The Timid Child"   *"The Unknown Ex"*

Lucinda Talbot = Marcus Talbot
"The Scary Aunt"   *"The Enigmatic Uncle"*
❖ **Joey Talbot**
"The Artistic Kid"

Naomi Kinnunen, Bugs Fletcher,
Anna Stuart, Orv Anderson...
"The Honorary Grandparents"

Ad infinitum...

=	Married
≈	Separated
÷	Divorced
❖	Children

Lavinia Hoope Hansen

The North Shore of Lake Superior, late 1800s

*C*avinia Hansen had a notion. It dropped oddly out of the sky one warm afternoon as she sat alone in a high clearing above the lake. From a distance, she was a small figure seated at the center of a ring of bluffs. Up close, she was a petite and lively woman who watched with curious awe as, along the shore to the north, the shelf-like front edge of a thunderstorm moved out from land and across the water. The storm did not surprise her. All day the weather had been ripe—the morning bright and calm, mid-day sultry. It was toward dinnertime when the storm front moved in. Low to the horizon, gunmetal gray on its underside, the cloud trailed smoke and was coming in hard—gray replacing blue from north to west across the horizon.

Even among the modern women of her acquaintance, Lavinia was intrepid. She was as comfortable on the musky windfall cedar beneath her as she would be in a parlor. Her hair, graying mahogany, was caught up in a bun. Strands were fallen, heavy with heat. She pushed them back without thought and scribbled a line into a small ledger, then closed the book. Her brow furrowed. *Why doesn't he return?* Her husband, Henry, had gone off walking and could be anywhere beneath the leafy canopy, which stretched newly green down the long slope to the

1

lake. Lavinia hadn't wanted him to go. He had promised he'd be brief, but she knew. This was their first look at the land as owners, and Henry, being Henry, would forget. He'd be distracted. They hadn't quarreled, but Lavinia knew they'd not parted well.

The thought stayed with her as she waited, impatiently—then, chiding herself, patiently—then impatiently again. The first hour had become a second, and her impatience turned to worry. Where was he? She scanned the clearing's edge. No one. Nothing. The line of brush and tree curved unbroken.

She expelled a slow breath and shifted her attention back to the storm. As it neared, the light of day was changing, becoming at once sharp and muted, the broad face of the bay stippled with highlight and shadow. Lavinia, too, was distracted. Eyes drawn to the play of light and texture below, her hand patted at her skirt pocket. There. The hard circle of her watch. She withdrew the hand, turned her eyes again to the tree line. They were eyes expressive and dark, like the eyes of an animal.

A push of wind, cool, as abrupt as if a door had opened, set the sugar maples that bordered the clearing to lifting their palms then bringing them, shuddering, down. The sound of branches sifting wind rose, fell, rose higher around her. With each pulse, Lavinia felt growing urgency.

Suddenly, in the midst of it, she heard her name. "Vinia."

Her mind leapt. *Vinia.* Only he called her that, only Henry. She turned to where she'd heard his voice, listened for the cracking of brush and watched for his long stride to step him clear of the undergrowth, axe hefted to a shoulder, revolver safely tucked away.

Lavinia, too, carried a firearm. She glanced at the long barrel next to her, leaning against the cedar, and the earthy scents of the clearing were cut through by the smell of morning bacon in the pan, of wood smoke and the faint odors of snow melt and first green shoots outside the open cabin door. They were smells from the first spring of her marriage. She'd been at the stove, turning bacon, when her ear caught a vibration. She glanced at Henry, who looked up from the table. Their eyes locked, and the vibration became sound, the heavy gallop of something winter-starved, drawn down the hill path to the meat curling and snapping in her pan. She watched Henry's slow leap for the gun where it stood against the wall an arm's reach from the bed, heard the gun's roar, felt her nostrils sear with hot powder, and then, the heavy stench of the bear as it thudded across the threshold. Blood ran *swoosh rush swoosh* in her ears.

The memory was dispelled by a low moan of thunder.

Lavinia scanned the tree line. It was far past that spring. She'd only imagined the voice. No one was there. She passed her hand over the skirt pocket again.

Lavinia knew—she was not like her husband. Henry had eyes for distance. She saw the particular. Earlier, she'd examined the clearing, back and forth, had collected every detail and written them into the book. She closed her eyes and listened to the wind in the trees, its tug at her ears. In her mind she saw a picture—in this place, a white house, green shutters, and she herself picking peonies beside a picket fence. Huge whites, vibrant pinks, drooping on the stem, like infants in her arms.

A beating of wings, a nearing din, brought the moment to an end.

Her eyes opened, her head tilted back. Above her, against a sky gossamer blue, a flight of birds was assembling. Large and white, powerful, they merged into a turning circle above her head. Her breath caught. The birds formed a rotating crown—a moment later, seemed pearls on a string. One snip, and they might be flung off and away. Lavinia had never seen such birds—only their feathers in ladies' hats, their images in books—and if she had, she wouldn't have expected an exhibition like this.

Short of leg, bright orange of beak, the birds were pelicans. Careening overhead, they rode a draft that swirled and dipped. The great wings, ten feet from tip to black-fringed tip, turned in slow arcs. The pebbly voices called rhythmically out. Each bird cast down at Lavinia one comprehending eye, and as they wheeled above her, eyes flickering and turning, she was cut free from the earth and lifted up into a living web.

In the southern sky, more pelicans appeared. As if on cue, three birds in a tight V-shape, a blazing arrowhead, spun in and melded with the circle, just as, like a single entity, the others began to peel off and disappear above the trees. Disarray erupted overhead as the circle unraveled and thinned. Seven eyes, flickering overhead—four, three—until the last strange cries of the pelicans wove away beyond the treetops.

Lavinia stared into the empty sky. Within her, a glimmer was rising, something remembered. As she waited for it to assume a shape, she raised a hand to her lips, counted, without counting, each breath. At last, the glimmer became sense. The pelican, the bird that loves . . . As if they had some purpose, as if they knew my name. . . . *Where is he? Why doesn't he come back?* She pulled from her pocket the cool, reassuring watch, a gift, a keepsake, wrapped it momentarily around with her fingers and opened it. Quarter past four. She ran a finger across the inscription:

Lavinia Hoope
Confirmation Day
"Neither the day
nor the hour."

It was then that she had her notion—the word she would use for the rest of her life—a notion, delivered of pelicans, that this plat of ground on the breathing rim of the lake was hallowed. Closing her watch, a decisive snap, she rose and began to search. She wanted a mark, a token, and she combed the near parts of the clearing—under the prickly blackberry bush, around each rock and windfall, in the shifting shadow of the ash. Only when rain began to fall did she give up. She tucked beneath the root ball of a downed aspen and hugged her knees to her chest. Not a trace of pelican had she found, not the smallest feather, not a hint of scat. But she didn't keep her vigil there alone. As she waited for Henry, a circle of feathered angels moved unseen overhead, they kept watch with her. They were part of her now, the pelicans—heavenly messengers, raspy of voice, with eyes that flitted and turned, inside and above her head.

Eyes that were free, and intense.

Eyes obliging, wild, joyful.

Getting Where They Need to Go

*T*he town was quieting, the day winding down.

On the raised strip of concrete out front at the convenience store, a cluster of teens drank Diet Coke, they laughed, and blew smoke. Tendrils rolled along the plate-glass window, dissipated into haze. Between exhalations, the kids jostled one another or looked fixedly into the distance. Their eyes were caught occasionally by the headlines of announcements hanging in the window. The unembellished MEETINGS OF THE COUNTY BOARD, 1995. In a swirling script, FALL BAKE SALE, from St. John's Episcopal. A balloon-bordered CHILDREN'S STORY HOUR, Saturdays at the library. Side by side on the same horizontal sheet with, in up-tempo script, ESL CLASSES, MONDAY NIGHT. And, right beside the door, the announcement no one in town needed, FISH FRY, RAIN OR SHINE, FRIDAYS AT THE VFW. The store's neon lights had come on, and the kids looked washed-out under them. It was windy, an autumn wind, but their coats were unzipped.

The main street was bustling, folks getting where they needed to. Some walking, some in cars or vans, some in pickups—it was a small town. The young mother strapping her toddler into a car seat, the white-haired gent settling his wife into the passenger seat and easing shut the door, the new mechanic at the Ford dealership stepping up into her shiny F-150—all were glad they didn't have to drive the traffic of some city. This was peace. Something they would not give up. Many were born here. But more and more had come from somewhere and managed to make a place for themselves.

The door of an aluminum-sided building slid up and an ambulance, looking from above like a child's toy, rolled out. It turned on its lights, merged into the street, and raced across town. Heads turned, vehicles moved to the curb as it passed—the siren wailed, strobed lights popped like old-style flashbulbs against the approaching night.

On the rim of bluff above town, backlit by the last hint of twilight, the wind vane on the peaked roof of a church turned in fits and starts. A storm was coming, but it was still at a distance. Along the northern margin of town, and to the east, the lake stretched. On a far point a lighthouse shone, misleadingly small.

Above it all, unaffected by time, flew the pelican.

Serena Cross

*T*he chill outside lifted mid-morning, just before ten.
By ten fifteen, the day had gone to hell. But before we go
there, let me say the morning started out like any other. I slipped
into my nubbly-but-soft red chamois jacket, descended the narrow back stairs of the parsonage, and crossed the church
grounds to the cemetery. There's something about a cemetery
I love, and about this one, especially. In the sunshine this morning, the clutch of worn and fusty headstones rose brightly out of
a crazy quilt of leaves. Mostly maple—feverish red, calm yellow—
with a smattering of oak—crisply, patiently brown. As I sat there,
thinking, looking out over the lake and running leaves through
my fingertips, the world was kept at bay by the wrought-iron
fence that wraps the perimeter.

My favorite marker is Lavinia's. I could describe it with my
eyes closed or even find it in the dark. The stone is light-colored
granite in a protective iron casing. Some family member—I like
the idea of a blacksmithing nephew—must have added that more
recent touch. From the top of the casing, long since oxidized
black, projects a cross, a cross empty and lying on its side. On
the stone itself, a lamb in weathered outline sleeps. Its carved
front legs fold daintily beneath its chest, and it floats above a
four-line inscription:

Lavinia Hoope Hansen
Wife of Henry
October 13, 1848
May 10, 1932

Today is her birthday.

She's been gone more than sixty years. But when I sit beside her grave, I feel her. I hear her quiet breathing, see her lips quiver suddenly into talk. There's no one left to tend her gravesite, so though we've had frost, I brought flowers, the chrysanthemums that were so cheery on the shelf above the sink. The mums were in an applesauce jar. To keep them upright, I spaded a hole to drop them in. The soil was cold and hard, but I felt like working it with my hands, so I did. The rhythm of my fingers, the pleasure of moving and loosening and breaking apart, was calming and satisfying. I was alone, wholly private in my thoughts, and I felt good. Somehow I knew Lavinia Hoope Hansen would like yellow mums on an October morning.

As well as anyone.

*M*y husband, Richard, is pastor at Pelican Church, Lavinia's church, which makes me the pastor's wife. It's an unofficial role, but it's as demanding as anything Richard deals with. We've been here seven years. Richard's first calls were to churches in Wisconsin, then South Dakota. We'd honeymooned at a ma-and-pa resort on the North Shore of Lake Superior. Our cabin had low water pressure—the shower spurted and dribbled and reduced us to laughing tears when we tried to take a first shower together. But the view of the lake was so mind-blowing, we didn't care. When the call came for Pelican, it felt like it would be a second honeymoon—the lake, the pretty little church. Richard loves little churches, so like families, with their eccentric casts of characters. I was in need of a honeymoon. It's hard to do what we do. This glaze moves into people's eyes when they find out Richard is a pastor—the shutters go up. I'd like to thread my finger through their top buttonhole, give it a yank, and say, "You think we're milquetoast? Got nothing worth hearing? Well, stick around."

I wonder what people would say if they knew that my confidante, the one I go to, is dead, long before I was born. I hate to say this, but . . . the living . . . well, they're so much work. Take my women's fellowship group. Now, I love those women, each so different, such a life force, but . . . good God, what a garden of roses and thorns.

There are two women's groups, actually. The one I'm part of is married ladies and widows—the singles started their own group. We meet in the church library. It's so comfy and warm in there and smells like old books. We mostly just be together and talk, around food, of course—it's a church, there's always something yummy. We talk mothering, which is hard, and what it means to be married—harder yet—and, of course, we talk about faith. Don't get me started on how hard that one is. Most of our women have jobs and will make it to an event but not the regular meeting. At our last gathering it was the core group, mostly older. We got onto how our days fly by and we don't have time to pee or do our hair, let alone be aware of—well, what we should be aware of. We fall into bed at night not having spoken a meaningful word, some days hardly thinking one.

Now, having said that, before the meeting I had been thinking a lot about something, and I'd come to the meeting with an idea. I was watching for the right moment to bring it up, then my friend Toni got on a roll. She's an academic—she loves an elaborate plan. She hijacked the discussion. It was all I could do not to snort. Pastors' wives aren't supposed to snort. I was just about to say, "I've been thinking," when Judy Holsapple said, "When I was young, I was going to do so much. I *did* do so much. I know I should pay more mind to what's going on with me, but . . . I'm tired."

Bea Markowski laughed a little half-laugh. "Tired," she repeated, "I know tired." Bea does know. She's caring for a husband with dementia.

Anna Stuart was there. Anna is the biggest sweetheart, and she had this pained look. She said, "It seems like things get harder, they get faster, all the time. I don't like to turn on the evening news, and I think sometimes I should cancel the newspaper. I don't, of course—you know I wouldn't—but add it to everything going on in my life, and my head spins." She leaned toward Bea and patted her hand. "Does your head spin?"

"Ice," Naomi Kinnunen said. "You need ice."

Naomi's lifelong friend, Bugs Fletcher, was out of town, so Naomi and Mabel Gunderson were a pair. They'd been having a long side conversation—first about the time someone taped the communion pitcher shut on Jack Grange, Richard's predecessor, then about the perils of piecrust. Naomi's comment about ice was so amusingly timed, we all burst out laughing. Naomi said, even louder now that she had an audience, "I had to tell Elizabeth—I said to her, 'Use ice water.' Poor woman. Her crusts are dreadful."

"You are so right," Mabel said.

Everyone knew who they were talking about, and some of the ladies started tittering. Then Lucy Talbot let fly. "Your head only spins, Anna? I spend my days with a tornado in my head—going a hundred directions at once." Lucy is . . . well . . . that person who makes folks head for the door.

Anna's head visibly spun, just a little. She's used to Lucy.

Mabel was still talking piecrust. "Did you tell her," she said, "about not rolling a crust more than once? Someone needs to talk to her about that, too," and then she said, seamlessly, "Lucy,

I don't know how you do everything you do. When do you sleep?"

Toni had been listening with half an ear. She sat bolt upright and slid forward in her chair. "Let's do something about it," she said.

We stared at her. Do something about Elizabeth? About Lucy's sleeping?

Toni didn't notice. "I want to go back," she said, "I want to take us back to where we were saying . . . we were saying we don't pay enough attention—you know, to what's meaningful." She turned to Anna. "I'm happy, Anna, you're not going to throw away the TV. We need to stay abreast—local news, world events. The problem isn't what's going on out there, it's what's not going on in here." She touched her hand to her heart, then her head. "It suddenly occurred to me what we should do. We need to stop living on autopilot, the way we do. We need to be mind-ful—where we are, and where we've been. So, how about this? Before our next meeting, let's each write down some of our story. A mini memoir. And then let's come back and share them."

"Share? Out loud?" Anna said. The expression on her face was, *what now?* Toni gets that look from the ladies a lot. Anna shook her head. She said what all the ladies were thinking. "I couldn't. I'm just Anna, from nowhere to speak of. And if I did have anything worth telling, my words would tangle up. No, no. It's not for me." She turned to Lucy. "But you, Lucy. You'll have stories. Your life is . . . glamorous."

Lucy, digging in her purse, snorted. It might have been affirmation.

Toni's forehead had crinkled into furrows. She said, "Now, wait. Anna, you've lived through the Great Depression, World War II. You're going to tell me you don't have even one story?" She cast an eye my way. "Tell her, Rena. You're the writer here. Everyone has a story." All I could do was nod, because she never stopped talking. "Everyone is a story, in a larger narrative, like a panel on a quilt. I'm not talking fancy here. A lot of us like patchwork. We like running a finger across Aunt Hildy's paisley housedress, we love dozing off wrapped in our corduroy jumper from first grade." She was practically levitating off her chair. "Your words will come out just fine. Take stock of your life. To yourself, at least, admit what you hope. Come right out and say what you fear."

Mabel is married to the undertaker. I don't think she was thinking about piecrust when she said, "Ohhhh. No."

"If I lived where you live," Judy said, "I wouldn't want to think about it, either."

That's when Orv Anderson's silvery mop-top appeared in the doorway. He rapped on the jamb and said, "Excuse me, ladies. How are you all today?"

Blessings come in many disguises. "Good," I said. I was happier than I should have been, I suppose, that he'd derailed Toni. Maybe I could get a word in. "Toni was just convincing us we need to change our lives."

"No, no," Orv said. "You're good, just the way you are."

Orv runs the men's group. Now, the guys do a lot, but the fact is, when someone around here needs something—a pan of bars for a meeting, a congregational meal, a female eye for re-designing a space or redoing the landscaping—we're the ones they come to. Once a year, during the Christmas season, the guys make a gesture. They cook and serve a women's breakfast. That's why Orv was at the door. He said, "So—the sixteenth. It's good, for breakfast?"

We all looked at Naomi. "The sixteenth is good," she said. Anything having to do with food is Naomi's call.

When Orv left, the ladies started filing out right behind him, and Toni's mini-memoir plan deflated mid-stroke like a kid's water ring. Of course, I didn't even get to float my idea. I'd wanted us to do something to remember Lavinia on her birthday. She's in the church cemetery because she was a founding member, *the* founding member. The church exists, it got its name even, because of her.

So much for that—the day came, and all she got was mums.

*C*ike everyone who lives along the shores of Lake Superior, we're under its spell. In college, we used to drive up when we heard the smelt were running. The trunk of Richard's junker overflowed with buckets and nets. We'd bring hot chocolate and coffee, and we'd build a fire on the beach. The stars were so intense, the air so clean. Toward morning, we'd drive back to school and go straight to campus or straight to bed.

Superior. It's the perfect name, synonym for huge, changeable, tempestuous. Some days, the surface stretches inviting and tranquil, a benevolent deity dominating the landscape. Others, it turns choppy and dangerous, angry little whitecaps building to huge, famous swells. I swear, the color of the surface changes by the hour. It'll be a shade of slate, or turquoise, or aquamarine—then it turns red, rusted-fender red, when the wind blows hard and churns up iron in the shallows. There's iron in my shallows, too. Growing up, I walked iron-red roads, jumped iron-red puddles, breathed iron-laced air. It's no surprise, I suppose, that a lake buttressed by iron, criss-crossed by freighters carrying iron, draws me so.

*M*y father was an engineer for the Colgate mine, which sent its spidery veins deep beneath our house. The neighborhood, called Colgate Location, had the look of a mining company town—row after row of small, square houses terraced like mushrooms over Colgate Hill. Our house, larger than most with an open front porch running the width of it, stood out like a portabella in a patch of button mushrooms.

Mom and Pops had devised a timeline by which their only child was to reach the major milestones. They're a piece of work. After my young lifetime of being guarded and forbidden, when it came time to prepare me for the responsibilities of womanhood, they pushed me off the dock. I turned fifteen, and the next day Mom announced it was time for me to start babysitting. I couldn't have been more surprised if she'd told me I was going to be a big sister. Before long, I had a number of families relying on me, most of them folks around Colgate.

Before dark one Friday in early November, I walked up the hill to sit for Dottie and Bud Buckner. Theirs was the pug-faced house across from the abandoned Colgate Hospital. It was a reasonable place to sit, with mindful children, color TV, and the latest romance magazines, which Dottie freely offered. At our house, true romance was strictly contraband. My mother would have pitched a fit if she'd seen me reading it. I'd have heard, "Serena Amanda Leann"—they must have known they'd only have one kid, since they gave me so many names—"what is that in your hands?" What the Buckners didn't offer, but I had discovered, was girlie magazines in a kitchen drawer. Even Pops would have had a conniption about that. I looked at the pictures with a kind of hunger, wanting to be grown up, like those brave, naked women, flipping the last magazine shut with a vague sense of danger.

"Lock the door," Dottie Buckner said, and I dutifully did. The boarded-up hospital made me nervous. The keys to the Buckners' doors—skeleton keys, like at our house and every house—had been lost, the locks never updated. Anyone could have gotten into just about any house in the location. That thought never left my mind. After Dottie and Bud exited through the back door, which was in a windowless alcove off the kitchen, I slid the flimsy bolt across and snapped it down.

At ten o'clock, the cuckoo whirred out of its little hut above the couch. The kids were long asleep, and I was deep into the story of a woman in love with a man about to take vows as a Jesuit—a girl likes the thought of besting a worthy competitor, and you can't get any worthier than God. Just as the heroine was stepping from a cab to confess all for love, the phone rang.

"Rena. It's Dottie." Her voice was tight. "I need you to do something for me."

"The dishes are done."

"Thank you, dear, but no, not the dishes. Bud and I . . . we've . . . we've had a fight. He took off in the car, so . . . I'm waiting for a taxi. Here's what I need. If he shows up before I do, don't let him in." There was silence. I could tell she was considering what to say. "You hear me?"

"Yes."

"No matter what, don't let him in."

I promised. By the time I dropped the phone into its cradle, my fingers were ice. What did she mean, I shouldn't let him in? How could I not? I stood an eternity by the back door, thinking how flimsy it looked, how little the bolt. If Bud Buckner knocked at that door, I knew all I could do was pretend to be asleep, way off in the living room.

Anxiety lends to the ears an eerie sort of vision. As I stood beside the door, willing Dottie's cab safe transit and speedy passage, my ears saw the tires that rolled into the gravel drive. They saw the turn of a wrist that cut the motor—so, not a cab? My heart dropped and began to pound, *no, no, no, no,* and then the slamming of a car door, and footsteps. Footsteps heavy, too heavy and slow. Finally, the creaking arc of the storm door as it opened on the porch. I slid to the side of the door as if I might be invisible there, my back to the wall.

More steps, then three thick, assertive raps hit the door, followed by dead air.

The porch floor creaked under shifted weight. My body had slowed to the speed of wood, all but my heart and my brain. I was leaning into the wall so hard, my spine was two-by-four and plaster.

More raps, harder, louder. Three raps, four. Then again. Then car keys clattered to the porch floor.

"Shit."

It was Bud, for sure—Big Bud, Mr. Buckner. He leaned down to pick the keys up, and his shoulder hit the door. He cursed, rattled the knob, and hammered so violently that the wall behind me rumbled and rocked.

It suddenly stopped. There was silence, except my breathing.

"I know you're there," Bud said. His speech was slurred, his voice wheedling. "C'mon. Unlock the door." He paused. "Jes' reach up an' push back the bolt."

I was so freaked out there was no logic to my thought. *He sees me, feels me, right through the door.* My mind leapt. What would he do if I didn't let him in? Or if I did? I backed up harder into the wall. A night sky had bloomed inside my head, and constellations were wheeling in it. My muscle and blood began to shower sparks.

Bud Buckner punched the door once and shouldered it hard.

"Open the go'damn door!" I didn't move, didn't breathe, didn't take my ears off the skinny bolt rattling in its sleeve. "Bitch," he muttered. The porch door slammed. Finally, I heard his engine gunning, all the way down the hill.

Only then did I begin to shake.

When Dottie got there, she was embarrassed and terse. "I'd walk you home, but if he comes back, he'll lock me out." She pressed four one-dollar bills into my hand, though she owed me only three.

Beyond the porch light, out of Dottie Buckner's sight, I started to run. A pack of Colgate boys roamed the streets at night. Something about it made people nervous—that something that, if she thinks about it, makes a girl afraid. There had been incidents. Something—no one was sure exactly what—had happened to a girl in an old mining-company shop building. I ran like hell down the cold dark stretches between streetlights, my breath pluming against the lights farther down. I flew, terrified that hands were going to hook me from behind, too terrified to blink. My heart was crowding my tongue, and there was a poker in my side. Streetlight after streetlight, I didn't let up or let down until I was in striking distance of my own yard. Just as I thought to relax, a cigarette flared in the dark. I stopped short, squinting, my breath heaving in ragged gasps.

"Serena?" It was my father, sounding surprised from where he was seated on the step that connected our walk to the city's. "What are you doing out there? Those people didn't drive you home?" Pops gathered me and took me in, whereupon my mother had some choice things to say, most of them to Dottie Buckner over an icy-hot telephone line. I never sat for Buckners again.

I've replayed what happened that night again and again and concluded that, fifteen or no, the situation was one that allowed no good way out. As frightening as the episode was, it left no lasting ill effects. I've never forgotten, though, that the one I trusted sent me out into the dark.

Of course, maybe Richard would offer a few thoughts from his perspective on the ways in which I am warped. "We're all a bit warped," he says. Small consolation. Fortunately, I have Lavinia for comfort. She liked to keep track of things. Our first year here, Richard and I read her account of the church's origin in a history I found wedged beneath the drawer of an old desk. Naomi and I had taken on the balcony storage room on spring cleanup day, and we discovered the desk under a mountain of junk.

Naomi's a brick. She's got her hands into so many things. She's one of those women no church could survive without. She has the soft, double-folded eyelids of an older woman of her ethnicity—Finnish, as many here are—and the comfortable demeanor of someone who's been a member most of her life. She knows her way around the place. Sanctuary, sacristy, kitchen, nursery, library. From the loftiest loft to the smallest nook or cranny. Naomi was married at Pelican. Her children, all eight of them, were baptized and confirmed, her daughters married, at Pelican. Except, of course, Esther, who's the radical of the Kinnunen bunch and ran off to St. Paul. Naomi's parents and even her husband Einar, last April, were buried through Pelican. She has her own funeral plotted out, right to the placement of her casket—carved mahogany, she'll have you know, the scene from the Last Supper—and the composition of the floral arrangements depending on the time of year. She's informed Richard her hymns are to be "Rock of Ages" and "How Great Thou Art," and rumor has it she's given Mabel a list of women to serve at the luncheon. She's allowing Richard to decide for himself what to say in the eulogy.

"I think you know me well enough by now, Pastor," she said, one Sunday as the coffee hour was winding down.

"Why, thank you, Naomi. I think I do, after all the Lenten soup and sandwich suppers you've prepared, and the thousand urns of coffee."

"And the new member receptions."

"Those, too. You take the prize for tater-tot hot dish."

"Of course," Naomi allowed, "Bugs helps me with most of it." As I said, she and Bugs were in diapers together. You see one, you'll see the other. Bugs's real name is Borghild, which her little brother couldn't say, hence Bugs. "Except," Naomi continued. "That time her gallbladder went bust and she dumped the mother-daughter dinner on me with a day's notice.

Not that I didn't pull it off." As Richard nodded sympathetically, she said, "If you live long enough, things happen. You handle them. I just want you to know, Pastor, I trust you not to embarrass me." Which meant, of course, she didn't trust him at all. Even bricks have their idiosyncrasies.

"Oh ho!" Richard laughed. "Is that how it is? Well, thank you again, Naomi, but I'm generally more worried about embarrassing myself."

Naomi had never seen the history before. "My word!" she said, whatever word she was laying claim to clearly on the outskirts of profanity. "Floyd—" she said, wheezing with humor at the picture in her head, "Floyd will be drooling worse than Scout when he gets wind of this."

We shared an understanding laugh. Floyd is our church historian, whose clumsy but affectionate English setter has sparked life into many a gathering at Floyd and Carol's place, moving from knee to knee, resting his head to stare up adoringly and leaving horseshoes of slobber. I don't know how Carol can stand to live with that dog.

I took the history home and sat down with a cup of Darjeeling. The book was thin, clearly penned when there wasn't much to record. The paper, once white, had gone to beige, curled in places, and smelled strongly of dust, of heat and of damp. Thin though it was, it felt full. As I held that slender volume, I felt every funeral, every wedding, every christening it had been witness to. I had a sense of every sermon, as if I were hearing them simultaneously from a distant room, a hushed, intricate weaving of voices.

Lavinia's story, coming across the years in her own words, put her at the table with me. Church lore is that she and Henry didn't have children, something that, before my first pregnancy, I lived in fear of for myself. Even after I got pregnant, I waited for things to go wrong, especially carrying the twins—no one dodged more petrochemical bullets or sidestepped more electromagnetic fields than me. When I finally held Andy and Scott, and then Chelsey, in my arms, I was able to let go of that fear. But I found new things to obsess about. As someone famous once said, the unvexed life is not worth living. Or something like that.

Lavinia's father left her an inheritance, which she and Henry used to buy some land. Their acreage had a crow's-eye view of the big lake and was heavily wooded except for a clearing that edged a rocky bluff. Lavinia had been born among the hills of Massachusetts, so the spot above the lake spoke to her. What she wrote about it made her seem as alive and real as any woman I know: "I had a notion to build a white house with green shutters, plum and apple trees blooming all around. That notion was replaced by one, sudden and certain, that arrived on the wings of pelicans."

Lavinia had never seen a pelican except in naturalists' sketches—then she saw not one or two, but a flock. She was out on the new land, waiting, who would guess, for Henry, when a migratory group swooped in on the winds of a storm and circled above her. She had some sort of mystical experience. She was a reader of folklore and knew church tradition. As the birds flew off and she gathered her wits, she remembered the pelican was a symbol for Christ. That homely bird—clumsy, top-heavy oddity—is said to love its young so deeply, it pierces its own body to feed them with its blood.

Now, Lavinia claimed her word was enough for Henry. She told him what had happened. The two of them talked, they prayed. In the end, they took it as a sign and gave up their own plans for the land and donated a parcel of it to be the site for a church. The congregation they belonged to was discussing a purchase of land, and Henry and Lavinia floored the assembly by rising and, hand in hand, offering the prime section of theirs.

People then were as likely to shoot pelicans as celebrate them, between wanting the feathers and competing for fish, but the strange story of Lavinia's pelicans had gone through town as if on the birds' own wings. People wondered, were the pelicans sent by God? Were they God, a manifestation of God, in some mysterious way? The congregants, every last man and woman, accepted the Hansens' offer. When the church finally stood above the lake, its sanctuary doors opening onto the water, Lavinia spoke at the consecration. She observed it wasn't the house of which she had dreamed, but one the land shaped. God's house, built literally on rock—yes, on a bluff, which she thought the Divine Wordsmith must get pleasure from. A house of rock. The congregation was a practical bunch, and they'd raised the walls stone by stone from glacial rock dug out of their fields. In remembrance of the pelicans—birds that to this day gather on breeding grounds to our west—the members gave the church its simple, peculiar name.

Pelican Church.

People say Lavinia's pelicans never left. Some claim to have seen them, or to have seen one—a single pelican, in the distance or overhead, watching, then sometimes right up close. Is it possible? Is it one of the pelicans? I don't know. I'd like if it were. People try, we try so hard, to find something, a connection—human, maybe, or divine—and we mess up. Boy, do we mess up. What I do know is that, because of those pelicans, a lot of lives have been affected, in good ways, when they've most needed it.

In the early days, the church stood alone above the lake, with what's now the downtown area below it. As settlers arrived, they built up the hill and into the area around the church. People have always found its name odd and interesting. They've been intrigued by Lavinia's notion of pelicans on a mission for

God. Over the years there have been—well, nobody knows—countless commemorations of the birds' visit, from t-shirts to art. After the Second World War, a couple celebrating their golden anniversary commissioned a metal sculptor from the South Shore to create a pelican wind vane out of copper. It was mounted above the vestibule door in the spring of 1947. Ever since, the little fellow has looked out over worshippers as they come up the walk. The Property Board, affectionately known as the Pelican Polishers, hasn't been up there in a while, and he's turned a little green from rain. He stands there, jaunty as all get-out, with one wing slightly raised and his short legs straddling the peak of the roof—the north, south, east, and west symbols beneath his feet slightly out of kilter, his spinning and pointing registering some perpetually wrong direction.

I spend time with Lavinia often. Out in a cemetery, I find relief.

Truth is, there are days I'd like to secede from the human race. What with working more now that the kids are in college—I clerk the front counter at the Assessor's Office and there's no fully explaining the pleasure that is—what with the unglamorous duty of running the house, the . . . the tedium of being the pastor's wife, I can be, on any given day, crushed. Lord help me if I forget I promised to bake bars for some meeting. The flinty irritation or bruised hope in people's eyes makes me leave the meeting inches shorter than when I arrived.

Lately, I've been hanging by my nails from the empty nest. Scott and Andy are worldly sophomore men this year, back home at Houghton Tech, and Chelsey went off this fall to be educated by the Lutherans. Taking the boys to Houghton wasn't as hard as taking Chelsey to Concordia. Chelsey's a PK, through and through, a preacher's kid—more than the boys. I'm not sure if that's reassuring or scary. There are so many pressures on clergy kids, which she's handled to this point, but she is in the throes of growing up, and I worry that on her own she'll cross some irrevocable bound. When I think back to my own college years—well, there's this flush of heat. It's been perplexing as a parent as to how to guide my kids to safe water, without pretending I didn't take my own canoe through some whirlpools at her age. Chelsey's not at a hotbed of sex and radical thinking . . . still, a lot changes in those years.

The day we left her at school, she was buoyant with life, all hopefulness and light beneath her golden freshman beanie. Her eyes were wide, so dark like Richard's, her freckles muted by foundation but still discernible and precious. She modeled the beanie for us, and I couldn't hide a smile. Well, more a smirk.

"Okay," she conceded. "It looks dorky."

"More like we're three years old," spat her roommate, Merope.

Merope, a girl with a nest of unnaturally black hair, had come up from deep in a book. The look she had going was half Beat poet, half urban punk. It looked odd with her baby face. She . . . she unnerved me. I was going to leave my little girl with . . . this?

"You don't like your beanie, Merope?" I asked. Running through my mind was: *Merope. Merope Moffitt-Smith. People make some dumb-ass decisions. No wonder the girl is scary. Who would give their child a name like that, a name she'll be fighting all her life?*

Chelsey had recognized in the question my propensity, inherited from my mother, to egg people on. She doesn't share it— she's a chip off her father's block. "Mo-o-o-o-m-m," she said. She drew it out, warning me off by giving my name extra syllables.

"Yellow. Ugh," croaked Merope.

"Not yellow, gold," Chelsey said. She said it gently—she also has her father's way with people. "Merope," she added, "the color looks great on you."

Of course, in Chelsey's estimation just now, I'm in a different sphere than the rest of the world. She isn't shy about letting me know she thinks my status as a mother gives me a compromised grasp on higher things—I hate to think of the hard fall that's ahead for her, when she has kids of her own. She said, "We wear the beanies because we're part of something. You just don't get some things, Mom."

She was so earnest. I said, "I can't dispute that, I guess, or your father will step in and offer state's evidence."

"Church and state," Richard said, shaking his head. "Better they don't mix."

Chelsey hates when we banter at her expense. She gave us a look of exasperation and said, "I'm serious here. This beanie is . . . it's . . . well, it's tradition. It's got . . . meaning."

Richard took her side. He usually will. "Don't let your mother rile you, pumpkin. Enjoy your beanie, then store it somewhere safe, because as you get older, that dorky hat and everything it stands for will only get more meaningful."

Chelsey sent an unspoken *Thanks, Daddy* that lit her father up. Merope Moffitt-Smith glanced into the mirror as she adjusted her beanie, then went back to her book with a low huffing sound.

*N*ot long after, I'd done an about-face. The thought of driving away and leaving our baby girl was opening hairline fractures in my heart. Chelsey had gotten a primo room, in the dorm she wanted, a room she'd prayed for and sweated blood over. I looked around it. Starfish and sea horses floated across the crisp blue ocean of the comforter on her bed. Red towels and washcloths—she'd chosen red, she said, to enter her new life with flair—blazed on a corner of the desk, and the textbooks and notebooks purchased that afternoon glowed with potential next to them. But there in the midst of the new possessions, the signs and symbols of Chelsey the grownup, sat flop-eared, frayed-at-the-joints TooBoo, the teddy bear she'd lugged around since she was two. His brown, threadbare butt was planted securely in the middle of her pillow.

That did it. Fortunately, Merope had gone out for pizza with a young man sporting one earring and an orange mohawk. Something tight, full, and hot surged up the back of my throat and out my eye sockets. Chelsey's flooded, too. "Mom," she said—one syllable, all forgiven. "Don't. Don't make this hard."

"Who's making it hard? It's hard by definition."

Chelsey flailed across the space between us. "I'm going to miss you so much," she said. "I miss you already." Her warm, narrow, strong frame pressed into me, and I was filled with something like the awe I felt the first time her small redness lay squirming and burning on my chest.

"I miss you, too. I mean, I miss my little girl. But I'll be fine, and so will you."

With the two of us blubbering like we were, Richard almost lost it. A weird sort of spasm crossed his face, and he stared intently at an invisible something hanging in the air. His voice struggling—God help a man if his voice should break—he said in that gruff tone he seems to use more and more, "It's late, Rena. If we're going to be home before breakfast, we need to get on the road."

We walked to the car through this lonesome, searching wind blowing off the prairie. I cried half the drive home. It's been a couple months, and I'm still not feeling right. I stop, I listen, I think. Why aren't the tremulous tones of Lisa Loeb filling the house, all hours of day and night? Chelsey is crazy for Lisa Loeb. She'll play "Stay" over and over until we tell her to stop. All of a sudden—all at once—Richard and I were left with just each other. It had started to dawn on me, already last year when the boys left, that maybe being the two of us again wasn't going to be easy. It was nothing I could put my finger on. Then Richard got his pants on fire, and not over me.

When my parents chose my first name, they hit way off-mark. I try to live up to what "Serena" implies, but I don't. My friends tell me that from the outside I look as if I am—serene. But I know better. I may appear placid on the outside, but I'm roiling on the inside. If I live to be ninety, I'll never understand. The name thing again. What would prompt someone to give their child a name like that, to be a stone around the neck?

When I was ten, I'd had enough of it.

At the table one night—and it was night, since Mom liked to think of us as East Coast, and East Coast eats later—I caught my folks off-guard. It was one of those moments where nobody is talking. Knives and forks were scratching across our plates in imitation of conversation. My mother can get a bit intense, a quality I guess I inherited. To avoid being derailed over food in my mouth, I swallowed and said, "Pops. Mom. I don't like my name." They both turned and stared at me, mid-bite. "I want you to call me Rena," I said.

They exchanged a glance, the sort Richard and I have come to know well ourselves since we've been parents. Pops laughed, one of those *what's this?* laughs, and Mom placed her tableware down. A person will always notice my mother's tableware technique. Since our trip to England, the summer I was seven, she has held her utensils European-style—fork in the left, knife in the right. She dabbed her napkin to her lips.

"Very helpful, dear," she said to my father. Theirs is a marriage based on a battle of wills and ways. "As for you, Serena, eat your liver. Then maybe we'll discuss it."

"Now, Serena," Pops said. "You know you have my grandmother's name." His left eyebrow lifted hopefully. "Hers is that little portrait on the wall of Gram's sewing room. The oval miniature that will be yours someday."

"Howard," Mom said, taking her utensils up. "Don't bargain with your child."

Pops wasn't going to drop it. "It's a beautiful name. A family name. You should be honored that of all the women in the Capshaw family, you carry it. Rena sounds—" He stumbled, first for lack of words, then because, like me, he'd seen the look that had moved across my mother's face. It wasn't ominous, but imminent. "It sounds," he continued, "like . . . like somewhere you go to gamble."

"Or divorce," Mom said. She'd decided early in life that her birth on the Iron Range had resulted from a wrong turn on the part of her delivering stork. She popped liver wrapped in onion into her mouth, chewed seven times, swallowed, and followed with a single sip of burgundy. She's a little tightly wrapped.

"So they say," Pops said. He held his martini glass aloft—his third of the night, by my count—and said, "Serena, pass me the spuds."

𝓜y folks are rare for their generation. They're both college graduates. Pops studied engineering. Mom double-majored in English and psychology. They're pretty much mismatched, and come by their adversarial relationship honestly. What I know of their college days makes campuses in those years sound damn amazing. I'd like to have been at one. The GIs had just come home—battle-honed hard-asses moving into dorms with freshmen right off the farm. During the war, Pops was in the military police. He's proud of having served, justifiably. He's also interestingly proud of the way, once back in the States, he and his GI friends intimidated the R.A. on their floor.

"I'd heaved guys bigger than me into the slammer, all over Europe," he said one day, "and this beardless kid thought he was going to tell me I couldn't smoke in my room. Jesus H. Christ, we took care of him!"

Mom was reading the *New York Times.* Her voice leapt gleefully from the tent of its pages like a cat on a mole. "I wasn't aware the Lord has a middle name."

"Holy," Pops said. I watched in amazement—seeing his error, he was twisting in air, shielding his jugular. "The 'H' is for 'Holy.' Sorry, Serena," he threw my way.

"Horse shit," the *Times* retorted, with a jubilant shake.

Pops has always been fond of the saying, "There are no atheists in foxholes." He was raised Catholic, and still is, but he lives his life according to a to-each-his-own philosophy. When it came to my upbringing and religion, he deferred to Mom, and she saw to it that church was hardly mentioned. In our house, it was just an oddity that Pops would occasionally go off to Mass.

My mother's the atheist of the family. Her family—the older generation, I should say—were staid and careful Protestants. "I can't tell you," she'd say, her voice full with the fleshy tones of televangelism, "how many awful Sundays I endured." It had become a litany. "Poker-stiff, hands folded, eyes in my lap on a straight-backed chair, wa-a-aitin' on Jesus. Praise God!" she was fond of finishing. "A-men, and A-A-A-men!"

Life with them was . . . unusual. I was forever picking up—and in some cases putting right back down—all sorts of books that Mom had around. One day there would appear a novel that might as well have been in Sumerian, by James Joyce. The next, poems as good as Greek, by Ezra Pound. An accurate generalization about my mother is that the more complicated something is, the better she likes it—and she's given to saying outrageous things, just for effect. I remember a particularly interesting phase where she made loose with the work of Freud.

"That Maureen Brown," she proclaimed one night over leg of lamb, "wouldn't be so bitchy if someone would nail her good."

Mom was referring, of course, to Mrs. Brown's getting a little bedtime action, but what did I know? This was before sex ed at the Buckners'. I sat there, contemplating an alarming but pure image of Maureen Brown ten-pennied to the country club wall—hair a perfect beehive, the beady eyes and stiff tails of dead animals hanging about her shoulders. Ermine, Mom would always point out, not mink.

"I like Jim Brown," Pops said. "You like Jim, don't you?"

"Jim's all right. He left her, didn't he?"

Mom about drove Pops and me nuts with her eyebrow-raised analyses of everyone she knew, because he and I had to live in the same house and squirm right under her magnifying glass. Now, I'm not one of those people who can't or won't appreciate their parents' humanity. I love my folks dearly, but I'd have to be blind not to see their foibles. My father and mother are the most self-absorbed people I know. They've always been vague about why I'm an only child—I was either such a blessing, they feared another would be pushing their luck, or such a trial, they stopped while they were ahead. I never got to just be a kid. God help me if I scuffed my shoes or went out with uncombed hair. We never had visits from Santa or the Easter bunny, the way other families did, and the Tooth Fairy never left booty at our house. My mother's parenting philosophy was, "Children are better off raised to see things as they are." So I sped through childhood as the third Capshaw adult.

The small one with limited power.

The way they were raising me didn't sit well with the extended family. Pops's family has always been a little leery of Mom. They didn't dare say a thing, but her family made up for it. One night when I was around eight, her brother Bob and his family dropped by. It was a beautiful evening—the beginning of spring, warm and clear, too early for mosquitoes. My father had just bought me a book of bride-doll paper dolls, which my cousin Terry and I took out to the porch with two pairs of scissors. The adults got left to do what they always did. They spaced themselves around the squat-legged dining room table over coffee.

After a short, for the most part friendly discussion—something the school board had done, I think—Uncle Bob suddenly said, "I don't care if you get mad at me here, but I think you should be taking Serena to church. Or Sunday school, at least."

Now, the peculiar thing about my mother's family is, the madder they get, the lower their voices. Through the screen door I saw Mom's hands fly up in the dismissing gesture she has. "Oh, Bob," she said, her tone somewhere between amused and annoyed, then I caught the phrase superstitious tripe. She said, "All that blather about a ghost in a gale, tongues of fire, babbling in tongues. We're teaching her right from wrong, how to use a fork, for God's sake."

Uncle Bob said, "That's just like you, we're not discussing the rules of etiquette."

And Mom said, "It's only good manners, Bob, to keep one's bloody nose out."

I looked at Terry.

She moved her shoulders vaguely up and down and went back to her cutting.

I have to confess. My nose has never been very good at keeping itself out. I squinted through the screen. Uncle Bob was leaning across the table. He started in how my mother was self-centered, she was feeding me God-is-dead casserole and atheistic stew. The terms didn't mean anything to me at the time, but they were so odd, and everyone inside was so agitated, I made a mental note.

Aunt Louisa laid her hand on Uncle Bob's arm.

"Bo-Bo, calm down."

I like my Aunt Louisa. She was blessed at birth with a sooth-ing disposition she's somehow managed to carry over into late life. She said to Mom, "Really, Annie, she might take after her father."

Mom said, "Serena can make up her own mind, when she's older. For now, our Sundays are wonderful."

To my amazement, Mom was sounding as if she were going to cry, then she started calling Uncle Bob by his given name. That seemed more like her. In my experience, it's been an in-auspicious sign.

"Breakfast late, Robert," she said. " Long walks with the dog. Television and reading, Robert, and no end of time. No boring sermons, by boring old men. No sharp-tongued old bat in the next pew, praying, Robert, praying for the strength to make it through another week of chasing the neighbor kids out of her yard."

My father was noticeably quiet. He'd lit up a Pall Mall and was taking desperate drags from it.

Uncle Robert's voice became, unbelievably, lower. He said something about humanism—I filed that, too—and prejudice. He said, "You don't like anybody, Anne." Then he said to my fa-ther, "Why don't you step in?"

Pops waved the cigarette distractedly. He muttered some-thing about an understanding, about apples, not tipping the cart.

Uncle Bob threw his arms up. He said something I couldn't catch, and then Mom said, "Good riddance." She spoke the words slowly, with distinct separation. I knew she was livid. I could barely hear her at all. She said, "Drop it, Bob," then some-thing about my being able to take care of myself, charms and incantations worth less than shit.

From there, things disintegrated.

It was a night that ended with tears and chairs flung back from the table. They stopped short of throwing them. My aunt and uncle burst out the door, grabbed Terry by the arms, and dragged her off the porch. "Come on," Uncle Bob yelled, loud enough for the neighborhood to hear. "We're leaving." They jumped into their car, and you could tell by the way the gears shifted, Uncle Bob was really steamed. My mother went upstairs and disappeared into the tub. Pops gave me an apologetic kiss and evaporated out the door.

I sat at the table—surveying the half-empty cups, the cigarette butts—and fretted. But one thing comforted me. For all their differences, Mom and Uncle Bob were attached. I knew that, and I knew that no matter how mad they got, they loved one another. Next week, Terry and I would be out on the porch again. Mom and Pops and Uncle Bob and Aunt Louisa would be friends. That's not to say they wouldn't have at it again—they would, over some subject or other. They wouldn't be able to help it, being people who live in their heads. But it wouldn't be fatal.

As I sat there replaying the scene, something became clear to me. It was like a bell ringing on a February day. Mom couldn't keep me in a vacuum. I knew things from my friends, including things about religion, and from observing my own family, one thing seemed obvious. If we really are created in the image of God, then God is something else. I'll let anyone who's interested supply their own, more specific adjective. They can probably guess mine.

My entire life, I've been rebellious. While I was at home, I had to bury it, and for Richard I keep it on the QT. My favorite short story is by a man named Lees, a story in which the narrator calls God the Celestial Lunatic. The idea is, God's workings in the story's world are crazy and unpredictable. Well, hell. The world in the story is the same as the world I know, and I went around the parsonage for a week, reading sections out loud.

"Did you get that, Richard? Want to hear it again?"

"I fixed it. Last week."

This is typical, as our conversations go. You'd think a husband could at least half listen in the interest of world peace.

"Richard. You fixed it? I'm talking Greek, you answer in Latin."

"What? What do you mean?"

"Fixed it. Never mind, Richard. You fixed it. End of story."

Could you get any more oblivious? Of course, if the congregation were privy to this little scene, Richard wouldn't be the bad seed. The simple fact is, most parishioners love him. They look to him, they need things from him, a certain way of being. Not so with me. That makes me a liability. Though it's strained these days between the two of us, I've loved Richard a long time, and for his sake I tone it down, dress the way I should, and keep quiet about the things I think. When it comes to humor—don't even go there. With a few exceptions, the butts planted in the pews aren't there for yucks. A wrong joke can be deadly.

Okay, I'm ragging here, and on the hand that feeds me. It's not as bad as I've made out. I've got to give the congregation its due. Whatever their personal beliefs, the ones they don't tell the pastor about—and we hear things, we know they're all over the map—our group has a big heart for the world. There was a letter to the editor a while back, proclaiming Beelzebub had a pulpit in town when Richard invited a couple with a lesbian daughter to speak about their journey to supporting her. You've got to love letters to the editor. Some are perfect illustrations of lack of clarity. Richard showed me the paper that day and said, "So . . . who's Beelzebub? The speakers? Or me?" It didn't matter. Pelican turned out in force the day of the talk—all the heavy hitters were there. The show of support was gratifying.

At Pelican, we have one parishioner who can really curdle the lutefisk. I've already mentioned her: Lucy Talbot. She's pretty much a battle-axe, but she's not unlikable. In fact, there's a lot I admire. She's closing in on seventy but has the pluck of someone half her age. There's something sad about her husband, Marcus, but Lucy's a pistol. She's plainspoken, generous, and has a brassy charm. The Talbots are stalwarts at Pelican and, being business owners, mucky-mucks about town. They come from wealthy families somewhere down in Iowa. Lucy likes to remind people of that.

After all these years, a couple of Sundays ago she introduced Richard to a visiting friend. "Anastasia," she said, "I'd like you to meet our new minister, Pastor Cross. Pastor Grange retired, you know. He's been in Tollefson's since Mother's Day, two years ago—his Parkinson's got that bad."

Anastasia tsked and said, "It's sad when the good ones go." She bared her teeth sincerely at Richard and extended her hand.

It made me sigh. If a previous pastor didn't get run out on a rail, once they're gone, the congregation thinks they sit at the right hand of God.

Lucy's a mystery. I've often thought she must feel like tomcats in a sack—she has so many conflicting sides. She's a great supporter of the arts, especially theater, which confounds me, because she's so gloriously narrow-minded, it's hard to imagine subtle nuance meaning much to her. But she has her gifts. Last year one of our church families got hit by a lay-off and, the same week, learned their child had leukemia. Lucy went to work. She set up a benefit and phone appeal and made the hard calls herself. She had professional-quality posters printed, on her own dime, then dispatched the confirmation class to hang them around town. She sweetened the deal for the kids by footing the bill at the ice cream shop afterward. Money came in by the bucketful.

Lucy makes things happen. But her can-do spirit is paired with must-do vigilance. A couple years ago, the church hired a new youth director. Maya was peppery with energy, offbeat in a country sort of way. But in her youthfulness, she made an error in judgment. One night, she had the youth group line-dancing

behind her, singing "Boot Scootin' Boogie." The kids loved it—
they were whooping up a storm. Our three knew that Maya
would spend the rest of the evening in a church council meeting,
so when they got home, Chelsey dialed her home answering machine, and they all belted out the song. It was so sweet—the boys
had such crushes on Maya.

But Lucy Talbot had also been at church. She had passed
the youth room.

Oh, Lord. Maya got home and found a message from Lucy,
as well, one that sent her butt scootin' into low-earth orbit.
"Honest," she said to Richard afterward, "I felt the wind in my
hair. I saw the tops of jack pines falling away down below." Lucy
instructed her mightily as to proper tone and conduct for an em-
ployee of the church and advised her to shape up. And what
was good for the lowly goose was even better for the gander. She
cornered Richard in his office the next day for some instruction
and advisement of his own.

"Do I have to remind you, Pastor?" she said. "The Church
is God's representative on earth. Would Jesus go around jolting
and caterwauling like that?"

Richard accepts people where they are. He didn't see that
Maya was in the wrong, but he didn't see that Lucy was, either.
Well, except her tone. I had to agree. If Lucy was upset, there'd
be others. We're constantly monitoring. Yet others need to sing
and dance, so it's a struggle. Richard turned what happened into
a lesson for Maya on anticipating consequences, Maya ditched
the line dancing, and the activities of the Pelican Church youth
group took a more properly reverent turn.

In private, we shook our heads and laughed. A couple becomes used to such incidents when they're in parish work. People grow attached to the man or woman they share their pains
with. They consider the pastor a father or mother figure—for
some, the pastor is a manifestation of their better nature. It's

humbling. I mean, who could fulfill such expectations, deserve such love? The congregation remembers our birthdays and anniversaries. They've come out in droves to celebrate events in the lives of our children. And in times of illness or sorrow in the house, the parsonage should have a revolving door. When Richard's father died last year, offers of help sprang up like mushrooms and casseroles dropped by, numberless as the stars.

There's a negative, of course. "But we've never done it that way" falls from the tongue as naturally as "Amen." If a pastor does something in a way a parishioner wouldn't—makes a change to the order of service, schedules the children's Christmas program for afternoon instead of evening, allows yoga on the small-group roster—woe be unto her. Or him. It's poor Cousin Terry, dragged off the porch all over again.

Pastor and Mrs. Cross occasionally sleep in the buff—naked, not a stitch. One evening when the kids were still at home but spending the night at friends' houses, we indulged in some hot and loud sex. It was thunder and lightning, it washed every thought away. When Richard went to the bathroom afterward, he didn't bother with a robe. He even went down to the kitchen that way, to get us glasses of wine.

That's when the phone rang. I picked up in the bedroom to hear the voice of a young man. The fellow was saying he couldn't take it, not one thing more. I hung up, grabbed our robes, and went down to the kitchen. Richard had turned on the light next to the phone and was standing with the cord stretched across the room. Like a great featherless stork, he was balanced on one leg, straining to reach a dishtowel.

When he caught sight of me, relief flooded into his face. He said to the caller, "Can I meet you somewhere, so we can talk?" I held up his robe, and he flailed into it. "No trouble," he said into the phone, motioning for me to run and get him some clothes. "No, really, I wasn't doing anything important." While the incident completely unnerved me, he never broke his calm, caring, professional tone.

That's what was so attractive about Richard when we met. He was so steady, so much my opposite. The world could end this evening, and as the buildings fell, Richard would stick calmly to whatever he was doing. Not me. I'm descended from a long line of over-reactors and worriers. If worrying were an Olympic event, we'd own the gold.

Let me tell a story about my Grandmother Capshaw.

One hot, very dry summer in my late adolescence, Gram C. hired a crew to re-roof her house. One of the workers was a cute, charismatic boy of seventeen who inspired in me dramatically heightened concern for my grandmother. I came over early and hung around all day.

"Gram," I'd say, "can I get you anything?"

"No, thank you, Rena."

"Let's go sit in the yard. We learned in health class you should get a little sunshine every day."

"Is that what they call it nowadays?"

The boy said hello to me, twice, and ate a cupcake I'd decorated. I knew it was mine because there was a Hershey's Kiss on top. Gram hadn't put any Kisses on hers. "I'm not so loose as some," she said. Pretending not to have heard, I carried the tray to the dropped tailgate of the foreman's pickup as if I were approaching an altar. Then I sat on the porch swing, cradling a glass of lemonade and watching the boy eat. It was the supreme test of the adolescent girl's talent for watching young gods without actually looking at them. I'm afraid, though, I wasn't his only acolyte. Not long after, a girl a few years ahead of me in school met him at the altar, knocked up. It was a total bummer.

But that day, I knew nothing of that, and too soon, the roofers were done. While they'd been inspiring, the crew wasn't especially neat. They drove away and left the yard littered with cedar shingles, with tarpaper and wood. So as not to blow my cover—I've always been giftedly self-delusional—I turned to Gram and said, "I'll help clean up, if you want . . ."

She was elbow-deep in her blue-striped bread bowl. "Sweet child," she said. She turned the bowl upside down, gave it a whack, reinverted it, pulled dough off the sides with a rolling motion of her fingers. "Your father's coming tomorrow after lunch. Come along—and bring those Kisses."

The next morning, a radio show for early risers—one of those down-home, joke-filled, "here's what's going on" sorts of programs—reported hams on sale at the butcher's and a forest fire in the next county. It didn't matter that the flames were under control. Gram had never gotten over the memory of her family's house burning down when she was a little girl. A grass fire less than two states away would send her into a tizzy. Before the sun had the coffee pot on, she was pounding at our door.

"*Howard.* Howard Capshaw. You get out of bed, and get that girl out, too. We've got shingles to move to the rock pile before they burn the house down."

Pops tried to reason with her. "Ma," he said, "if a fire comes close enough to ignite anything in the yard, the house will be gone."

She wasn't hearing him.

"Every shingle, Rena," she ordered, pointing an arthritic finger. "Every stick."

I've turned out a lot like Gram Capshaw—don't know if it was learned, or in the genes. Richard's calmer style snagged me from the first. Now, that's not to say my husband doesn't have any balls. In his quiet way, he holds up his side of an argument. Believe me, I know.

When I woke up this morning—the morning that started so well—it was dark, in that decline-of-summer way, and I could hear Richard downstairs, puttering around. I could hear and smell the coffee pot doing its job. The day felt good. I lay in bed awhile and let the wiry bands that the years have wrapped around my heart unwind a little. Those moments are rare, but for an instant, I even loved perfectly. Loved life, loved myself, loved Richard and the children without expectations and without baggage.

Richard is a good man at heart, and I believe I'm a good woman. But the man who shines in the pulpit, who dazzles in the counselor's chair, is as aggravating at home as any other. Maybe that's the problem—he is my husband, and I know him so well. It drives me crazy when I see women in the congregation adoring him, some of them very young, very attractive. It may be sexy and exciting to dream of slipping between silk sheets— as if we've ever slept on silk—with an alluring man of God, but someone ought to set them straight. I would so like to back them, one by one, into a corner and say, "If you had to launder his socks, dearie, if you had to live with him when he's in a bad mood, you'd take your adoring ass somewhere else."

It's hard to stay civil—even harder not to snipe at him. Other folks can get away with broadsides in public, but everyone expects ours is a perfect marriage. Jesus, Mary, and Joseph. As if I need any more stress. I'm constantly reminding people that we don't live the way other families do. We work weekends and take Monday off, and all the big holidays are spent with the church. If Mom and Pops and Leona, Richard's mom, weren't so willing to come to us, we wouldn't have a family life. And forget friends— the pastor needs distance to do his job. It can be lonely. Some days, I feel as if the church is my rival—a doe-eyed virgin in a cashmere suit, a whore of Babylon with rainbow eyes and shimmering veils. Richard leaves early and comes home late, and many nights he disappears again after dinner. Meetings, he says.

Okay. He really is in meetings.

I can live with his being gone a lot, but what sends me is, he spends so much time talking to everyone about their problems, the last thing he wants when he gets home is to talk about mine, or ours. Or if I do get him to say something, he goes into counselor mode. With God as my witness! There's nothing as maddening as a lover who talks to you outside of bed like some impartial third party.

Sometimes I think the problem is we're both bullheaded. That, and the fact we married so young. We were twenty-one, barely. I'd have a heart attack if my kids wanted to get married at twenty-one. I can't help but think, it would have been better if Richard had been more . . . experienced. It's bound to cause problems if a couple isn't equally yoked. Sooner or later, they'll start resenting what the partner can't change.

A long time ago, another life, I imagined I'd get an advanced degree, then write a few books. The books my mother had kept around had done their work, and I had visions of myself at the bottom of a large lecture hall in a short skirt and patent leather boots, packing in the undergraduate masses to glean a fraction of my brilliance. But I never finished my BA. When Richard and I got married, I dropped out to work. I said, "I'll go back later." But before the first frost, I was pregnant, which meant both of us had to work. I've taken courses as I could, writing, mostly, but with Chelsey arriving eleven months after the twins and my continuing to work all through seminary, that was as far as I got. Somewhere in my thirties, I gave the idea up.

Richard knows perfectly well that my not making something of myself isn't only my doing. Still, he looked at me one morning, as I was enjoying a quiet cup of coffee and meditating over the daily crossword, and said, "I wish you'd done something with your life."

It stung. I couldn't believe he would say something that hurtful. I glanced up for a moment then looked back at the puzzle

to decide which of the complicated, conflicting responses lining
up in my head I should speak.

He said, "Don't you?"

I did, but wasn't about to say so. I looked up and stared him
down. "I did do something. I devoted myself to getting you
where you are."

It wasn't fair. It wasn't even accurate. Funny how we do that,
when it suits. I laid out my life's plan as much out of fear as out
of love. Romanticizing graduate school was one thing, but when
it came down to the actuality of it—real people, making
demands—I choked. Over the years I've learned not to dwell on
things spoken during low moments, and fortunately, Richard
does the same. Otherwise our marriage might have ended up
long ago where a lot of clergy marriages end—in front of a judge.

We were an unlikely pair. I guess I'm more like my parents
than I care to think. Religious life was the farthest thing from
my mind, and Richard ended up, as he likes to put it, at a kegger
he wouldn't have gone to except he was dragged by his house-
mate. They walked in and found an elf dancing on a coffee
table, long-haired, blonde, grooving to "Jumpin' Jack Flash." It
was me. I wasn't inebriated, mind you, not that night. Just exu-
berant. I was singing at the top of my lungs and kicking my legs
up, chorus-girl style. Richard says there was something fetching
about it, about me. I don't know—maybe he sought me out in-
stinctively, some part of him needing to loosen up. Maybe I
found myself drawn to him because of a spiritual side that was
starved. Maybe we were just in the right place at the right time.
Who can say how they ended up with the partner they did? All
I know is we fell in love—the Lunatic sense-of-humor at work.

We were juniors when we met. I'd crossed the border freshman year, to the University of Wisconsin's Madison campus. It
was the perfect place—secular enough to please my mom, radical
enough to please me. Richard transferred in two years later,

starting out at a small campus close to home. By the time he walked into that party—with his short crop of black hair, his averted, wine-dark eyes—I'd been, as they say, around the block. A couple of times. The first encounter I hadn't planned, exactly. I just sort of fell out of the gondola—the guy was older and an operator, and when it was over I felt as much relief as anything. The second, with someone I'd really lusted after, was more deliberate on my part. It lasted longer, and the breakup was harder to take.

While neither relationship ended very well, they'd been instructive. My sex education at home amounted to my mother handing me a small, yellow book with a chicken on the cover. Hens and roosters, a variation on the birds and the bees. Those first relationships were important—they filled in some big gaps. With AIDS and all, I wouldn't want to be looking for a partner now, but back then everything seemed so simple. Even sex. There's nothing simple about it, of course. But we were the last generation that had the privilege of being young and stupid in a less dangerous time.

When I got to Madison, I went to a clinic and got on the Pill. I wasn't plotting the life of a trollop. I just wanted to be prepared. I'd even managed to convince myself Mom had given her permission. She had, sort of. "For God's sake," she said the day I left, "don't get knocked up. Your father would make you marry the bum."

I blushed. I was so backwards about my sexuality, I'd used a mirror to figure out where the Tampax should go. The thought of anything bigger being welcomed into that tight place seemed unlikely. But even after I found out what a kick lovemaking was, and how much I liked it, I had no intention of settling down—not for the foreseeable future, at any rate—and I figured when I did, it would be with some guy just like me. Someone hip. Someone dangerous. Someone foaming at the belt.

Then I met Richard.

He was awfully cute, and even better, not of a disposition to pound on a door. But what a square, what a milk beard, what a babe in the bush.

What a challenge.

If life made any sense, he should have ended up with Toni, who was my roommate, but they were too alike to want one another. Toni was red-haired with creamy skin and looked like she'd just left puberty. She was also nine-tenths brain and about as uptight. She and Richard, when I first met him, were the only people on campus who could make Lincoln stand up. Not the real Lincoln, of course, but a statue, one with resolve on its face to make you teary. He's seated at the top of Bascom Hill, and if a virgin passes by, he'll give them a nod, lifting his creaking bones out of the chair.

Our first week rooming together, I hauled Toni into a lingerie shop. She stood staring into the dressing room mirror at the minimalist bra I was trying on. "You'd wear something that small?" she squeaked.

"Sure," I said. "But I'm actually thinking of giving bras up. Any together woman would." The look on her face was priceless.

Toni's another example of the divine law of opposites attracting. The whole time we were roommates, she wouldn't get it on with a guy to save her life. She blanched when I brought home a copy of *Our Bodies, Ourselves*. I, on the other hand, was all about guys. But that didn't stop us from wearing our hair the same—close as we could get, anyway—walking the same, talking the same. We began to think the same. Oh, and bleed the same. We were so psyched when our cycles merged. Even today, I'll hear myself say something and think, *That's Toni in my head.* Back then, she hadn't come fully into herself yet—she's got an odd sense of humor and a taste for the quick retort—but she already had her offbeat quirkiness. After Madison, we managed to stay in touch, or rather, I did, when she wasn't in one of her work frenzies and would answer the phone. Toni's the reason we came to Pelican. She called out of the blue one day, by then a big-shot professor. I answered, we chatted, and then she said, "Hey . . . I don't know what's up with you two, but . . . my church is looking for a pastor. I know Richard would be great, and it would be nice, having the two of you around. You interested?"

As roommates, we did everything together. Well, not everything. I obviously didn't take her on my *amours*. But when I was first seeing Richard, it was always in a group and she'd tag along. There were ice cream runs to Bascom Hall, nights of hot fudge pound cake sundaes at a little place on State Street. We owned a pew at a smoky bar next to the stadium, where we downed pitchers and ate brats to the music of folk guitar. Toni was a hoot—she'd get a little tanked and start to sing along. Richard would egg her on. "Thatta girl. Belt it out." I didn't know who was cuter. She didn't always go along, of course, and it was on one of those days—a warm September afternoon when it was just Richard and me, watching boats sail past the Union Terrace—that he finally held my hand. Both hands, actually, fingers clasped around plastic cups of beer.

Those first days were almost a religious experience, Richard and I playing dual roles. Initiate and priest. He opened me to the mystery of God, I opened him to that of sex. Don't get me wrong. I didn't go to church with him and roll to the floor gifted with tongues. My spiritual journey has been a gradual one, with occasional kinks in the road. I simply sat and took everything in—from the architectural beauty of the building to the smallest of things. The bowl of hyacinths on the altar, the candles with their hopeful flames, the rows of numbers crisp and squat and ordinary on the hymn board above the pulpit. I tried to look with Richard's eyes and my father's heart. Something had kept

Pops going to Mass all those years, and I wanted to know what
it was.

Richard came to sex the way Jacob met the Angel. He wres-
tled with it. Our first kiss didn't happen for over a month after
we were holding hands. While I waited, old-fashioned enough
to want him to make the move, I lamented to Toni daily. "Is
something wrong with me? Am I too thin? too fat? Should I
perm my hair?"

The day I said that, she was lying across her desk, one arm
lost in her natural curls, her nose nearly touching the pages of a
textbook. She sat up long enough to shoot me a *come off it* look,
then fell right back into the book.

I threw myself across the room onto her bed. "You think
he's gay?"

"He's gay." She didn't even look up.

"He's not. Toni. I'm trying to have a conversation here."
She still didn't look at me—she was studiously indifferent.
"Toni," I said. "I need you here. I don't want to waste time on
someone who's never going to make the time I invested not a
waste."

"Excuse me? Will you listen to yourself? A little rich girl
whining about only having a Ferrari."

"Oh, I see, and you're the truly poor girl? Well, I'm dying
here, and I get piss-ass nothing from you." I rolled off her bed
and, on the way to mine, turned on the TV. "You wait," I said.
"Someday you'll find out."

It wasn't one of our happier moments, but we survived it,
and the instigating problem resolved itself without anyone's help
or advice. Richard finally gave in, and the kiss was pure heaven.
From there, we moved in excruciating increments. Torsos
meshed in a slow, slow waltz, his hands making captives of my
breasts right through the layers of my clothes, our cut-off-clad
legs twined together on a blanket in the sun, the skin of our

thighs heated, active, perspiring. We inched forward, inched back, leapt forward, leapt back, until we'd worked ourselves to a pitch.

I wish, sometimes, we could go back to those days. Sex between us now is steadier, if rarer, the familiar drift and drizzle of tide on an ocean beach. That, too, has much to recommend it, but there are days when I yearn for that first vibrant intimacy, when each look, each touch, is an experience. Our bodies seemed more than they were, somehow. Sacred, almost.

No one had ever made me feel the way Richard did.

The first time he unhooked my bra—and he was all thumbs, so sweet—when it fell from my breasts, he inhaled sharply. "You're so beautiful." The way he said it, half in awe, half in pain, it was as if he were standing on holy ground, as if he'd breached the Temple veil. When we finally made love completely, one afternoon in the deep of January, we were bonded emotionally beyond the point of return.

Richard anguished so over sex, when he proposed on Valentine's Day, I took pity. I said, "Yes."

Toni seemed upset. She thought we were nuts and didn't mind telling me. "Have you flipped out? Rena, this isn't you."

"It's me now," I said.

We scheduled the wedding for June and spent the months in between in a dream. I'd never been happier. In fact, they were the happiest days of my life. Richard and I weren't burdened with the weight of life, yet we had promised to be. We were taking the steps toward growing up.

My only regret was Toni.

I had to pull away from her some, which gave me guilt. I'd made the mistake in the beginning of letting her rely on me too much. Her social life revolved around me, and I could see her alternately mirroring and needing me. I was so in love—and she

couldn't comprehend it. I think she resented it. I'd get this atti-
tude from her whenever I'd get back from having been with
Richard.

I was the most worried about her one Sunday morning just
before school ended. I'd gone away for the weekend to a
friend's baby shower, and I was so miserable away from Richard,
that I came back early, before breakfast. He was sharing the top
floor of a house, and I stopped at the dorm to get some books
I needed before I drove over and slipped into bed with him.

I figured Toni would be awake and gone. She loved Sunday
mornings—she'd go out and walk the deserted campus like some
earth sprite, smelling the air, sipping an extra large coffee she'd
picked up from the Union. I stuck the key in the lock—and
found the door unlocked. It gave me a start. I pushed it open
and the smell of a brewery wafted out, along with a strong smell
of vomit. The room was barely lit, the curtains drawn. I could
see Toni humped up facedown in her blankets, except for one
arm, which was draped over a trashcan that waited next to the
bed like a dutiful black dog. "Toni?" I said.

She groaned, raised the arm to wave me off, and groaned
again.

"Toni. What happened? What on earth? Are you all right?"

She brought both arms up to cover her head, moaned, and
mumbled into her pillow. My eyes had adjusted, and I could
see there was puke on the sleeves of her PJs, and clothes strewn
everywhere. It looked like she'd emptied her closet and
dumped every drawer. I said, "What did you say? I can't understand you." I sat on the edge of her bed, put my hand on the
small of her back. "Toni. What is this? You need to talk to me."

She half rolled and swatted at my hand like she'd swat at a
horsefly. "Don't . . . you, with your . . . your . . . You're the last,
the last person . . . I want to talk to." She flung back down and
covered her head with her pillow. "Just . . . go . . . away."

I never got to Richard's. I couldn't leave Toni in that condition. I sat on my bed in the dark until she agreed to get up, then I dragged her out to put something in her stomach. She turned less green as the hours passed. If she hadn't been so pathetic, it would have been funny. I mean, Toni, puking in a garbage can. All I could get from her was that she'd gone to a campus showing of *The Wizard of Oz*, run into some friends of her cousin's, and had too much cheap apple wine. I'd never seen such spit in her—it was like I was seeing a doppelgänger. And it stayed. There was something different about her after that.

Richard and I managed to get to our wedding day without any serious cold feet. After the wedding, we moved into a tiny efficiency apartment. It had one large window that opened onto State Street, and through it the smells of pizza and falafel drifted up and in—along with the din and diesel fumes of buses air-braking to a stop below.

We were happy there. We slept in an old Murphy bed that we stood on end every morning and swung into the closet. Richard watched, incredulous, the first time I went through my Capshawnian leaving-the-house ritual. "What are you doing?" he said as I unplugged the iron, the coffee pot, the lamp with the frayed cord. "Didn't you just do that?" he said when, having checked the burners on the stove, I went back and checked them again. It lost its charm, he said, about the second week.

What I learned that year was that I'd married the world's most fastidious young man. "Rena," I heard more often than I could count, "could you put your shoes away?" After twenty years, and three kids, we're pretty much the same. I still leave my shoes wherever I stepped out of them, and Richard still can get me back by pulling last week's leftovers out with a look of tribulation on his face. "Sweetie," he'll say, and I know what's coming just by the expression on his face. "Could we come up with some orderly plan for putting things in the fridge? Hmmm?" It makes me wonder if Lavinia wasn't fudging a bit, when she spoke of her marriage as if it were made in Heaven.

Lavinia. Did I mention that Richard tells me I have a tendency to digress? By the time I left the cemetery this morning, it was 10:15—time to make my slide into hell. I gave the mums a last arranging, wished Lavinia a happy birthday, and continued to the church. Life as a pastor's wife provides me no salary but compensates by way of hundreds of tasks. I washed my hands and stepped into the office to drop off an article that the church secretary, Amber, had reminded me I was supposed to write for the newsletter. I was leaning over her desk, interpreting my handwriting and explaining all the arrows, when the door to Richard's office opened.

I wished it hadn't.

Framed in the doorway, backlit by the window, were he and Claire Collier, and they were laughing, entirely too agreeably. The woman makes my blood pressure rise. She's young, pretty. I knew it must have been the end of a counseling session, and I tried not to look—Richard's a stickler about confidentiality. But I've got eyes. Any woman who's being honest will admit that other women sometimes scare her. This one scares me. She's going through a divorce, so the counseling is legitimate, I guess. But she's a strikingly noticeable girl—in a more primitive era, she might have worn a long bow and one breast—and she doesn't say a lot, especially around the ladies. She came to our fellowship gathering, once, and just sat there, watching, from under that dark sweep of bangs. It gave you the feeling she could be sitting on a powder keg. I do know this—she's part of a theater group in town that's famous for its actors' changing partners as often as they change scripts.

"You're flinging boulders again," Richard says. "For the love of Pete, take a look at yourself, yes, at yourself, and dredge up some compassion. People's lives are complicated."

Amber's eyes moved from me, to Claire, to Richard. I thought, *What's she thinking?* When Claire noticed me, her lips turned up into an odd almost-smile. There was something forlorn about it, and I could only wonder what it meant. But Richard's reaction needed no interpretation. When he saw me, he did a good imitation of Penelope, our lab, when she's pulled the bread bag off the counter again and you know from the look on her face she's been up to something before you even find the crumbs.

"Rena," he said. "Have a nice time with Lavinia?"

"Yes, thank you. Lavinia's well."

Richard rolled his eyes towards Claire. He said, "We can't keep her out of the cemetery."

"Better than trying to put her there," she quipped.

They all laughed—I managed a smile—and Claire said murder was on her mind. She's in a show right now where she's playing the sister of a very wealthy woman with a very new husband. "I don't want to give the plot away," she said, "but things aren't right with the couple—someone's out to knock someone else off."

Small wonder, I thought.

Claire smiled again, a full-out smile. I hate to admit, but it was like a flower opened. She said, "It's a fun play, a modern take on Shakespeare, a little Sherlock Holmes. There are secret passageways and howling mastiffs, a full moon and mixed-up identities. Curtain's at eight. I hope you'll all come?"

Richard smiled. The room was smiles, smiles. About when I thought I'd puke, he said, "We'll see. Just a minute, Claire. I'll walk out with you." He went into his office, reappeared, and handed his appointment book to Amber with a businesslike "I'll be at the parsonage, maybe an hour or so." To me, he said, "See you at home."

Lord knows what Amber was thinking. I spent the next minutes babbling about columns and sizes of print, trying hard to look normal. The whole time, I was working to lower my pulse, repeating, repeating my name, silently, as if it were a mantra. Serena . . . serene-a . . . serene . . .

I wasn't just being paranoid.

Well, maybe I was. But at times paranoia is called for. Just the other day, I read an article in the waiting area at the clinic that said the urge to be unfaithful is built into our genes. It came as no surprise to me.

It was last winter that Richard tipped the apple cart. We'd been having difficulty for a while, for no reason I could hone in on. It was just there, not overt, but a feeling, hanging between us, not spoken of. So I was both shocked and not shocked when, over first cups of coffee one morning the week after Christmas, he said, "I don't know what to do. I'm feeling . . . I've been . . . What I'm trying to say is . . . I'm finding myself . . . wondering about our life."

Silence pulled up a chair, dropped elbows on the table.

"Wondering about our life?" I said, at last. My voice sounded small, which was good, since the kids were upstairs asleep. My first thought was that he was . . . he must be . . . interested in someone, some woman. "Our life?" I said. "Don't you mean, wondering about some woman?"

"No, that's not it, at all."

"Oh?" I hissed it at him. "You need to find yourself, suddenly? You with the exact life you wanted, the life I helped you to?"

He cocked his head, kind of quizzically. "You're going to make this about . . . ? No. Wait. I see . . . this was a mistake. I thought it was something we needed to . . . no . . . I shouldn't have brought it up."

"Too late to put this horse back in the barn. I'll remind you—you were the one so hot to get married. Or have you forgotten? If I'd known then we'd end up here, having this conversation, I'd have taken Toni's advice and told you to bugger off."

He winced, turned his face away.

I wanted desperately not to cry. But tears welled and burned out in an intense flash. I said, "Yeah. The sad fact is, Toni saw both of us clearer than either of us did."

He said, "That may be. . . . Look, Rena. You're like marrow to me, you and the kids. But we've got a problem. You know it as well as I do." He uncrossed his legs, re-crossed them the opposite way, and looked out on the driveway. He said, "Whether you like it or not—whether you'll admit you have those moments, too—I'm feeling, so much feeling, I missed something." He was miserable, I could see it, and confused. And he was right. I've wondered more and more if we stay in this just because we said we would. But it's not a thing I'll admit to, or dare speak out loud.

We spent the next weeks being polite, civil, but only because we avoided discussing anything beyond garbage detail or who was up for chauffeur duty. There was a time I would have taken Richard at his word. Now I wasn't sure. There had to be someone turning his head. I walked around feeling heavy. Going over to the church, glancing into the sanctuary, killed me. I'd thought, *I'm doing my part, the Lunatic has my back.* Now I wasn't sure about that, either. I was alone, and there wasn't a soul I dared talk to. Not even Toni.

Truth is, Toni's hard to be around these days. She's a far cry from that girl covered with puke. In April, she separated from her husband, and since then she's been making up for lost time.

Her hemlines took a sharp north turn—think of her knees as the equator—and she's taken to wearing this obnoxious black beret. Worst of all, every time I see her, she goes on and on about her latest dalliance. She's a sociologist, so used to blathering she forgets who she's talking to. She sounds like the Great Poobah of Lust, like it's some religion she's discovered. She's got the zeal of a convert, complicated by the strange way people in her field view marriage. The strange way they view everything. Under all her kookiness, Toni has the softest heart—it's what I love about her—but, depending on how things are between Richard and me, her progress reports can set me off.

After the Christmas revelation, Richard and I didn't even go for counseling. Clergy have this tendency to struggle alone— I mean, who can you talk to without feeling like a failure? The weeks went by, the pain got duller and duller, we drifted farther apart. Finally, I don't know, I walked off the pier. When Cousin Terry's oldest daughter got married back home on the weekend before Valentine's Day, I went alone. Richard manufactured an excuse at the last minute, and Chelsey begged off because she had a date for a dance. "Mom-m-m-m!" she whined—I guess she was always masterful at dragging the syllable out—"I've been waiting for him to call since Christmas."

I didn't object.

Mom and Pops, I've got to say, were cool about it. They think the world of Richard, though a person might wonder about my mother, the way she rides him. The first time we let on that he intended to go into the ministry, she linked arms with him and said, "Now, Richard, was yours a calling on the phone? Direct dial? Or collect?"

"Uh. Direct."

"Hmmm. And your name is Cross. Isn't that interesting."

When I showed up without him, they had the graciousness, or the good sense, to act as if nothing were amiss.

It was an evening wedding, a typical February evening, icy and way below zero. The combination made the sanctuary a bit surreal, awash as it was with orchids and candlelight. The ceremony was beautiful, I guess, but for better or worse doesn't mean much when you're young. One moment, I'd be looking at the bride and groom and thinking, *You'll be sorry.* The next, I'd be biting my lip to keep from bursting into tears. By the time the pastor introduced Mr. and Mrs. Vranich, I had decided I was going to divorce the S.O.B. as soon as I got home.

I was sitting next to Pops. He must have picked up that something was wrong, because as the bells pealed and we followed the wedding party to the back of the church, he put an arm around me. "You're quiet tonight."

The wedding party was showering the newlyweds with confetti shaped like hearts. "Well," I hedged, "you know how weddings are."

I had the devil in my saddlebag that night. It turned out the groom's uncle had been in my homeroom senior year. He was one of a circle of boys I'd had a crush on—basketball jocks, every one. Incidentally, they don't make athletic uniforms like they used to. The trunks were short and sweet. I still get faint at the memory of straining buns over muscular legs.

Mr. Homeroom had become distinguished-looking—salt-and-pepper hair, an Armani suit—and very successful. He'd risen to senior partner in a Chicago law firm, at the regrettable, he said, cost of two failed marriages.

"Regrettable?" I countered. The word rocketed from my champagne-emboldened tongue. "Isn't that a double negative, regretting the end of something itself regrettable?"

"Been married that long, have we?"

"Long enough."

Our very cells were attracted. We danced and flirted, reminisced and flirted, drank and flirted—of course, being discreet about it. Afterward . . . well, there's really not a way to be discreet about this. We went to his hotel. He led the way in a candy-apple red Porsche he wasn't afraid to drive, even on ice. I could barely keep up. The entire drive, I kept saying to myself, "I'll go as far as the bar." But when he said, "Care to come up?" I heard someone with my voice say, "Why not?"

It was after four when I dragged my cheatin' genes home, feeling cheated myself. All the frigid slide to Mom and Pops', I berated myself. Not for what I'd done, but for the miserableness of my choice. The barrister had a briefcase-full of Trojans and lousy technique. Worse than that, I'd been a small cog in the wheel of his making love to himself. *If you're going to throw sense to the wind,* I thought, *you ought to at least have a wicked good time.* But I hadn't. The next morning at the breakfast table, Mom looked me over hard. Her instincts were blaring, but, for once, she didn't say a word.

When I got home, I couldn't do it. I'd remind myself constantly of my vow to leave—many times a day at work, during the Worship Board meeting, Stewardship Board, in checkout lines and in my car. I'd imagine swearing off God, scissoring myself out of the Cross family picture, but I couldn't. Something in me wanted to stay more than the other thing wanted to leave. So I hung tight. An unexpected development was, it wasn't so easy anymore to feel pissed at Richard. High ground had shifted.

One morning when I came out of the bathroom, I found him standing by our bed. He said, "Rena," and the floodgates opened. We wound ourselves up into a pretzel knot on the bed and cried. If we were going to make it, we'd need help, so we started seeing a counselor, a private one in a neighboring town. I can't speak for Richard, but from my perspective it's gone pretty well. Just when we seem to be back on track, though, something crops up, like Chelsey leaving. Or something in me will act out, and I don't know why.

I began seeing a second counselor on my own. I'd asked for a referral to a woman. Since I have days when I feel I should just run away, I figured seeing a man could be asking for trouble. Dr. Price advised an HIV test—which I got, with some finagling and good results. She also said, "You'll have to decide whether to confess the infidelity." I chose not. I admit. I'm a master rationalizer. Sometimes I justify myself with, "Richard couldn't handle it." Other times, I think it would be hurting him just to get my guilty ass off the hook. But there's more to it than that. A part of me is downright, secretly glad. There are moments when the knowledge that I broke faith with my husband haunts me—a man whose biggest mistake to date may have been he was too honest. Then, there are blinding moments when I don't regret it at all.

I had a few of those today.

For having started out so well, the day sure ended up on the dung heap. Just before dinner, Richard and I had a knock down drag-out over Claire Collier. Well, we really only had time to get started, but it was going to be bad. I was basting the roast, feeling a bit uneasy. Not long before, an ambulance had yowled by. It passed the house and didn't go very far before its siren cut off—trouble somewhere in the neighborhood. The screen door was banging, wind coming up hard. Just as I was making a mental note to get Richard to put on the storm windows, he walked in and leaned against the counter.

I glanced up. "We need," I said, "to put the storms on."

He nodded. "I know. I was just thinking it." Then he brought up the last thing I wanted to discuss. He folded his arms and said, "We should go to the play. It's important to Claire that I be there."

I closed the oven door and turned back to mixing a peach cobbler. "Well, good for her. Good for you. I'm not going." I told him, point-blank, "I don't like the look of it."

His jaw set, the way Andy's used to when he was small and I'd tell him no. Of the twins, Andy was the challenging one.

"It isn't what you think," Richard said. He stuck his hands into his pockets. "There hasn't been anyone, since . . . since we . . ."

"Since what?"

"Not anyone." He shook his head. "You're never going to let me off the hook, are you? For admitting—" A look flitted across his face, frustration, guilt, for feeling what he did. "That was a misstep I won't take again."

Something clicked in me, and I started at him with both barrels. "Good. Spare me. I don't want to know what else—"

And then the phone rang. Saved by the bell, an angel gets its wings. Richard shot me a pea-green look and went into the den to get it. He had on his pastor voice when he answered. It made me laugh. He said, "Oh, dear," listened for a while, then said he'd be right over. I knew it had to be a parishioner, and I was glad. I remembered the ambulance but shook it away. What were the odds? I'd won. He'd be tied up for a while.

He was so peeved, he left without telling me a thing—not who had called, or what had happened. Not where he was going, or when he'd be back. I was ignoring him, pointedly, but I heard the door close. It closed quietly—of the two of us, he's not the one for slamming—then the Mazda started. I got furious. I was filled with self-righteous indignation. *Go ahead,* I thought, *don't tell me. What do I care who you're with? At least I know who it's not.*

It was a very satisfying thought.

He hadn't been gone long, though, before I was reconsidering, before I'd dredged up a little remorse. I thought, *Serena Amanda Leann, you can be an idiot.* I started to think, *Maybe he'll go to the play without me.* I got this frantic feeling and started wondering if I should drive by to look for his car.

But I didn't.

I brewed a cup of chamomile tea and thought about calling Toni. But I didn't do that, either. I ran bath water as hot as I could stand and dropped in three pearly bath oil beads. Roses filled the air, an amnesic bloom. I stepped out of myself and into the tub, into the dog-eat-dog-eared world of *Wuthering Heights*—where I've been staring at the pages and wiping away tears, a wind as fierce as any from the Yorkshire moors rattling down the eaves of my heart.

Closer

*I*t was well past sundown. Night seeped into the cracks.
The kids at the convenience store had moved closer to the
door. Two girls shivered and laughed their way to a blue con-
vertible. They drove off, and a boy climbed into a dirty four-
wheel-drive with *Wash me* written on the driver's side window
and followed them. But others came. There was more laughter,
more smoke. When customers entered or exited with their lot-
tery ticket, their gallon of milk or dozen of eggs, the kids separated, then came together as before.

To the northwest, the storm drew closer. It pushed wind
ahead of it and carried sleet. It was on track to merge at the edge
of town with a train heavy with freight. At the cinema, late ar-
rivals for the 7:30 show knew sleet was coming but paid no
mind. It was to be expected, this time of year. They hurried inside. There was still time for licorice and popcorn, even a good
seat. That's the beauty of a small town. In line for tickets, everyone bantered about the first cold night.

On a street corner by the bus station, a human clothes rack
waited for a light. Its form was thick with layers, the sad total of what
it owned. Its face was hidden, covered against the wind, and it was
not clear if it was a woman or a man. A passer-by wondered, *Have
things come to that? And does it have a place for the night?* The
unidentifiable form crossed toward the station and disappeared.

On the wind above the wind, the pelican flew.

Cucinda Talbot

*T*hat damn Marcus.

Those were almost the first words out of my mouth. Funny. Looking back gives everything such a different slant. I'd told him to be home by five. We're patrons of the Larkspur Theatre—they call us "Angels"—and we were supposed to be at opening night cocktails at 6:30. I told him, "If you want to eat, be home early. Any later than five, and you'll have to go hungry." He went on buttering his toast, like he hadn't heard me. "Marcus, did you hear what I said?"

"Yes, Lucy."

Yes, Lucy. I got home late, myself—he was nowhere around. But it had been one of those days, anyway. The very first thing, the shipment of porcelain figurines I've been waiting weeks for came in—and two were broken. The spunky, pig-tailed girl in Little League blues had cracked her bat. The big-eyed cocker spaniel with the ruby collar had lost its tail.

I'd also done something stupid. Doing the schedule, I forgot it was Friday—Friday the thirteenth, I could add, if I believed in such things. I'd scheduled both Claire and Eva not to come in until eleven, and then Claire had to leave early. She's doing the play right now, and it eats up a lot of her time. I'm not begrudging her that, though. The girl's got troubles. Man troubles. It hurts me, to see how hard she's trying to find her way. "Go," I

61

said. "You deserve a little happiness. Besides, you're useless the day a show opens. God knows where your head is sometimes."

"I know," she said, "I love you, too."

"Don't be fresh. I'm your boss, I'm older, and may be better looking."

Claire laughed. I love her laugh. She's a pretty thing, with skin like marble. I don't mean stony-looking, but that kind of glow. She walks in a room, and the men in it climb over each other to get her what she needs. Once burned, though. Twice shy. None can reach her. They're trying to hold smoke.

The schedule snafu did leave us shorthanded much of the day. So, of course, every damn shopper in three counties had to decide today was the day to get just that special gift. And they expected us to tell them what it might be, though not a one of us has ever seen or talked to Lovey Cakes, or Sonny Boy, or Darling Girl, or tone-deaf Aunt Elvira. Sometimes, I get tired of it. I'd like to say, "Who gives a bleep? Give the young whippersnapper a boot, give the old broad a bird. Or better yet, flip 'em all the old canary finger and have done with it."

But I don't feel that way every day, and anyway, you can't talk like that and stay in business. So no matter how bad my mood, I at least try to look interested. If they're shopping for an older person, I smile and say, "How about this lovely pillbox in fourteen-carat gold, or this lap throw, imported from Sweden?" If it's a teenage girl they're shopping for, I'll say, "Have you considered a miniature blown-glass unicorn? Or a baby whale? Teenagers adore them." You've got to target your market—have a little poet, a little used car salesman, in you—if you expect to succeed.

I was in such a hurry when I got home, I didn't even pull the car into the garage. Lorna had already gone for the day. But she'd left her mark. I unlocked the front door, and the odor of roast chicken wafted out. I kicked my aching feet out of my pumps and said a prayer out loud. "Thank you, Lord, for plush carpeting and good cook-housekeepers." Lorna's the greatest. The table was set for two. A spinach salad with poppy-seed dressing waited in the fridge. The potatoes were peeled and sitting in a pan of water in the sink. I poured off most of it, threw the pan on a burner, and checked the phone's answering machine on my way up to change. Of course. He hadn't called.

"That damn Marcus," I said, out loud.

Leave it to Marcus to pick a day like this, one where we've got to be somewhere, at a certain time, to pull some kind of stunt. I'm not one to quibble with the Lord. But some days I wonder. Why'd He put men and women in the same galaxy, let alone the same house?

My mama shed more tears.

If you ask me, she was too beautiful. Mama was a slip of a woman, about five-foot-three, less than a hundred pounds, and she had unbelievable hair. It was thick but soft, and when she took it down, it hung in waves down her back. That hair had multiple personalities. If you ran your fingers through it or brushed it for her, you'd find shades of blonde and dark, with a trace of auburn to boot—straight hairs and curly ones, fine hairs and unruly ones, all mixed together. I loved to stand behind her and run her hairbrush down the length of it, watching her face in the mirror. Back then, Mama always had a surprised look when she saw her own face. Like, somewhere between frying morning eggs and drying the last supper dish, she'd forgotten how pretty it was.

Too pretty. That wasn't her fault—but once the bus has mowed you down, whether you were in the street or on the sidewalk doesn't matter. All Mama ever wanted was to be a good wife. I heard her say it a hundred times. But she had a run of rum luck. If you ask me, she was destined for it. Not only was she beautiful, she was sweet—and that was her fault.

My daddy was pretty, too. Lord, how we loved him. He was tall and dark, about six feet, I guess, with broad shoulders, strong arms and a face like a cherub. But his best feature was his smile. I've got this thing for smiles. Daddy had a hypnotic face all on its own, but when he smiled, the heavens took notice. He seemed to glow with this boyish light that life couldn't put out. And life was doing its damnedest in those days.

I was three when I really started remembering things. We were in the Depression then, and everybody we knew was rowing the same boat—if you can imagine so much rowing in northern Iowa. The thing Marcus and I have always loved about life up here is the water. At night a person can sit in our darkened great room and watch the lights of freighters gliding past out on the lake, chugging off to some port in Canada or on over to the St. Lawrence Seaway. What we looked at out the window in Iowa was tillable land. Mama was born a Southern belle, then her family moved to Iowa. She married Daddy at nineteen, and they set up on a little farm. It was a few acres, a few cows, a few chickens and pigs. Things were hard, so hard that Daddy took to going off to look for work. He'd hop a train and be gone for a spell. There was no shame in it. A lot of men rode the rails back then, and I'd bet Daddy wasn't the only married one. The important thing was, he always came back.

The farm was off the main road next to the tracks, and Mama and I would see hoboes walking down them every day. Hoboes came to the house all the time, asking for food. Sometimes they'd do some odd job for Mama, sometimes they'd just eat. Some of them, she let spend the night in the barn. Nowadays you'd have to wonder if you weren't letting some pervert in, to practice God-knows-what on your cows. But back then, it wasn't such a problem. People could still believe in the milk of human kindness. Mama would always say, "We've got to share what we have with the less fortunate." But she didn't let me talk to the men much. I always wished she would, because I wondered if they hadn't seen my daddy, or if they had a little girl of their own in some far-off place like Des Moines or Sioux City. I minded Mama, though, without question. If I didn't, she'd settle into her rocking chair and call me to kneel in front of her. I had to place my hands on her knees and keep them there, while she looked into my eyes and scolded me. The words seemed to go right into my soul. She didn't need to do more.

It seemed like I was always waiting for things—which maybe explains why I'm not one to wait for things now. When I was about five, the most beautiful dress in the world hung in Harriman's for what seemed like forever. It was blue velveteen and had a white satin tie that went almost to the floor. I wanted that dress. Mama kept saying, "It'll go on sale, Lucy. You've got to learn patience." I learned patience until it was coming out my ears. Every time we went into Harriman's, I held my breath. I dreaded the day we'd go in and find that some other little girl's mother had bought my dress. But then, mercifully, the price came down to two beautiful dollars.

And, of course, there was Daddy. We were always waiting for him. We never knew when he was coming. We'd hear footsteps on the porch, the door would open, and there he'd be. The times when he was home were like a holiday. I'd pull down the few books we owned, and he would read to me. Mama got younger and prettier—she hummed a lot and got this mysterious smile on her face. In the morning, she'd float out of their room when she went down to start the fire.

From where I'm sitting now—and in my mind, we couldn't get much softer—I can hardly believe those years were in the same century. Mama canned everything, from green beans to applesauce to meat, which in summer was hard to store fresh. Compared to how we live today, everybody roughed it. The only bathrooms we had were outhouses, aromatic old things the neighbor boys tipped over every Halloween. For light, people burned kerosene—it was dirty, stinking stuff. But what I remember most is bath nights. I miss them. Daddy would drag the big round tub next to the stove, and then he and Mama would put into it the water heating on the stovetop, then add cold water to make it just right. "You first, Lucy Belle," Daddy would say. Then, when I was done, Mama would get in, and finally, him.

All of us in the same water.

I wish Mama and Daddy could see this house. They would be amazed. Marcus and I have our own rooms with attached baths, each with a separate shower and tub. Marcus's is the master bath. The shower in there is a walk-in, sit-down affair with dual showerheads. *Good Lord,* I thought when we moved in. As if an old coot like him had even a prayer of luring someone in there with him—unless it was a home care nurse.

Even with Daddy going off to find work, he and Mama couldn't make the payments on the farm, and we had to leave it. We moved to a house in town, and that turned out to be okay because Mama and I had less to do when Daddy was gone. They sold all the livestock except Araby, our youngest cow, so pretty and red with a white star between her eyes. She made the move with us, into a stall Daddy fixed up in the back shed. Every day, Mama and I milked her. I think Araby liked me best. She stood very still as I pulled at her teats and let me tuck my head up along the warm underside of her belly. I could almost do the whole job myself. Mama only had to step in and get the last few squirts. In the evening we walked door-to-door selling milk, the pail balanced between us like it was brimming with gold.

One thing I'm sure of—coming out of a background like that, you know when you've got it good. You appreciate a windfall. Candy was a rare thing in our house, but my best friend, Mattie Hastings, was never out of it. Her family was lucky enough to still be out in the country, and the Baby Ruth

Company rented advertising space on her father's big round barn. How I envied Mattie that barn. As long as the ad was on it, the company kept the Hastings supplied with boxes of Baby Ruths. Lucky for me, Mattie wasn't stingy.

Marcus and I have always tried not to be stingy, either, which is why we were going to this fancy reception tonight, which we were about to be late for. *Criminy, where can that man be?* I thought. I zipped up my new black dress and called the east side store. I run our novelty and gifts business, while Marcus runs the liquor stores. We've got three of them, so he can be hard to find if he wants to be. Gary, the manager, got called to the phone from unpacking a shipment of Argentinean wine. "Boss man came through about three o'clock," he said.

"You haven't heard from him since?"

"Said he was going straight home . . . Say, Gordy, you want to check this lady out? This one—she's first. That's okay, ma'am. Okay. Sorry, Lucy. What was I saying?"

"Marcus. You haven't heard from him."

I could picture Gary doing an ill-at-ease shuffle, trying to figure how to not tell me something, or how to convincingly not tell me something that he couldn't because he didn't know. I waited. Finally, he said, "What can I tell you, Lucy?"

I let him off. "Yeah, I know. Thanks, Gary. If he shows up, tell him I'm waiting on him and I'm not getting any younger."

Marcus and I have been under a truce for years. I thought, *Okay, he stopped off at the bank or something. It's not the end of the world. I'm not going to let him get my goat over this.* I plucked my Cuban heels off the rack in my shoe closet—even a grande dame likes to wag a few tongues—and hurried down. I'd do my part. I'd have dinner on the table when he dragged his sorry ass home.

I dropped the heels by the front door and sprinted for the kitchen. For an old biddy, I can still move pretty fast. I tied

Marcus's Kiss-the-Cook apron on, lifted the lid from the potato pot, and on the strong smell of the spuds shot back to the worst year of my life. 1933. My breath stopped. My pulse soared. I stood back and watched Mama lift the lid on her big cast-iron pot.

The bubbles were rising and breaking around the potatoes as she pierced them. I heard a knock at the front door.

"Get that, Luce, will you?" Mama said.

I was just turned six, and happy to help. "Yes'm." I skipped from the kitchen into the front hall. It was Daddy's brother Jess and a stranger. Uncle Jess introduced the man. "This is Mr. Cudahy, from the railroad."

By this time Mama had joined us, and they said to her, maybe she should sit down. She said, looking scared, "Why?" and when she didn't move, Mr. Cudahy said, "I'm sorry, Mrs. Matusek, 'ma'am. Your husband's body was found on the tracks down in Muscatine County. Looks like—I'm sorry, ma'am. It looks like he fell off a train, got caught up under it."

Mama's eyes clouded over as he spoke. She started to shake. She fell to the front-hall rug and hunched into a little ball. Then she started flailing at the air. Uncle Jess dropped to his knees. He held her wrists and talked low to her. Mama started to wail, then, and say Daddy's name. "Al, Al, Al." She didn't stop.

That's when I couldn't stand it. I turned and ran through the kitchen to the back porch. I scrunched up sideways in the swing and pressed my hands to my ears.

I don't know how long I was there, but suddenly, the house smelled of something burning. The water in the potato pot had boiled away, and the potatoes had seared to the bottom. I saw Uncle Jess come into the kitchen. He wrapped his fingers around one of the metal handles, then pulled away quick. "Damn!" he said, hopping and sucking. When the pain wasn't so fierce, he pulled the pot to the side, using his shirttail for a potholder. Even when the pot cooled, it stunk to high heaven. Uncle Jess carried the whole shebang out and threw it in the alley.

Marcus and I drove by the house last summer. The place was a mess—the window glass was gone, the doors were off. It occurred to me that potato pot might still be out there, right where Uncle Jess dropped it. But I didn't look. You know how some things in life stick with you? I found out later Daddy had been naked from the waist down when they found him, that a train will do that to a body. I was married for years before I could bring myself to boil up a pot of potatoes. Marcus had to do it. The smell of the damn things cooking gave me horrible shivers.

Marcus. Where was he? I put the lid back on the pot and shrugged off a bad feeling. I checked my watch and kept thinking about Daddy. After he was gone, I missed him terribly. And if that wasn't bad enough, from that day on, I really lost Mama, too. At the wake, she threw herself onto the casket and shrieked she had nothing to live for. Grandmama pulled her off and glanced at me sitting between Grandma and Grandpa Matusek. She said to Mama, "Mind what you say."

Mama went into a spin. With Daddy's death, the life went right out of her. We spent the first couple weeks after the funeral at Grandmama and Grandaddy's, and when we did come home, Mama would lay on the bed and not get up. My older cousins came over morning and evening and milked Araby, and they took over carrying the milk pail around. I begged Mama, "Let me go, too," but she refused.

"You're too little to go without your mama."

"M-a-a-a-ma."

"Lucy, don't talk back."

I sat there and watched her get smaller. She even stopped caring what she looked like—and that was scariest to me. Her beautiful hair got dirtier and messier. I'd try to brush it and could hardly get the bristles through the tangles. They were bunched up like a hornet's nest underneath. Mama would put her arms around me and say in a voice I hardly recognized, "Poor baby, lost her daddy. Poor baby. Poor, poor baby."

She wasn't the Mama I'd known. She scared me, and she scared other people, too, I guess, because Grandmama and Grandaddy came over one day and took us home with them. Some farmer bought my beautiful Araby for a song. Then every trace of life with Daddy was gone.

I think I started to see, then, what a woman could become if she loved anyone too much. Maybe Mama was just weak-spirited and would have gone a little off even if Daddy had lived. I don't know. But I figured out early on, a person would do well to be wary—just in case—and keep from getting too fond.

Alone at night in my room, I started thinking of myself as the Roman goddess Diana. I'm not much of a reader, except an occasional romance, but one of the books Daddy used to read to me from was about the gods and goddesses. I pictured myself snapping a golden whip, driving Diana's chariot, or sprinting across the fields, bringing down pheasant and white tails with a shining bow and arrow. I especially liked that Diana was goddess of the moon. Those winter nights the first year after Daddy died, nothing seemed as strong to me as Lady Luna, hanging naked over the world behind that round, unpierceable shield.

With Grandmama tending her, Mama came back to health. She wasn't ever her old self, but if you hadn't known her before, you mightn't have noticed. A couple of years later, she got married again. That didn't make me very happy. I couldn't stand the man. Well, I guess I liked him okay at first. But she went too far. She tried to make me call him Daddy.

"He's not my daddy," I said. I dug my heels in, deep.

Before Mama could call me to the rocker, Wallace stepped in. "Don't push the girl. She can call me anything she wants, long as it's not Asshole to my face."

That's how Wallace always talked, even when I was around. After he married Mama, he moved us to a nice-enough little house on the outskirts of town, right next to the Byerly brothers' place. Out our back windows, we could see their big fields of corn, row after row of healthy green stalks stretching tall and promising from the edge of our yard farther than a girl could see.

Wallace could be like a drop of honey on your tongue, then turn into a bitter pill. Mama was pregnant and not having an easy time—her body weakened at the same time as her mind. She was in the outhouse one morning, heaving her insides up, when Wallace marched across the yard. He was really put out, and yanked the door open. She was kneeling with her head hanging over the hole, and he snorted and said, "When you going to be done in here? I need some hot water, to shave." Like she was having a facial or something.

"I'll be in. I'm just a little slow this morning."

"More like every morning. I don't understand you. My ma birthed twelve and she never made a stink out of it. Forget it. I'm going to town."

"What time you want supper?"

"When I'm ready. Think you can handle that?"

God forbid he should get a bottle in him. One Sunday toward the end of Mama's pregnancy, he sat at the table all afternoon, downing whiskey. Mama tiptoed around him and talked real careful. When she started to get dinner, Wallace said, "I don't want no supper." He got up and sidestepped out. We found out later he went to the local still and drank some more. He came home just after ten. Mama and I were sitting together at the table, playing cards and listening to the radio, when he stumbled up the porch stairs and tripped over the threshold. He landed smack on his nose.

I knew better than to laugh. Mama and I stood up and grabbed hands. We just looked at each other.

"Waddaya lookin' at?" Wallace said. It was like he'd never seen either of us before. He picked himself up, sloppy-like. "I'm tired of the way you females treat me. An' I'm tired of not feelin' welcome in my own house."

Mama pushed me behind her. "Now, Wally, you don't know what you're saying. We're always happy to see you. Aren't we, Luce?" She prodded me with her elbow.

I nodded. "Yes." I was telling a lie, but I learned early that a lie can sometimes save you.

"Hell," Wallace said. "No other man would put up with what I do. You gotch'er nerve, keepin' a goddamn shrine in the front room. A goddamn altar to goddamn Al Matusek." Wallace lurched past us and started for their bedroom. "I'll blow the godda—" He hiccupped. "Go'damn miserable thing away." Mama and I knew he meant business. He was heading for the closet where he kept his guns.

"Wallace, don't," Mama begged.

He kept going. Mama grabbed me, and we bolted like rabbits for the front door. My heart was pounding, it was going to jump out of my chest, and I could only imagine what Mama's was doing, carrying so much baby. I grabbed the offending picture of Daddy and me off the front room table on the way out. It had been taken the last Christmas. I was wearing the velveteen dress. Daddy had on a white shirt and smart-looking vest.

We didn't have any neighbors close—in later years, I'd think Wallace planned it that way—so there was nowhere for us to go except out back to the corn field. Mama pushed me in ahead of her. She was frantic. "Faster, Lucy—go. Don't you dare stop." We half ran, half crawled, until we were deep in the field.

Thank God, Wallace was too drunk to follow.

"I'll kill you bitches," he yelled. He repeated it half a dozen times and fired the shotgun blindly into the field.

"He'll be all right," Mama said. Her arms were around me, and I felt her shaking. Her hair was unpinned, falling in our faces. We stayed there all night—even after Wallace went inside and probably passed out. Mama kept saying to me, but really to herself, "He'll be all right. You'll see." But she didn't sound sure, and in the morning, after Wallace had somehow got himself off to work, we crept inside and packed. And that was the end of Stepdaddy Wallace. Mama and I went back to Grandaddy's and never left again.

After that, I couldn't abide the smell of soil anymore. Laying in it that way for a damp eight hours, I wouldn't help Marcus in the garden for love or money. "Marcus," I'd say, when he'd ask, "I'd sooner pay for my flowers and produce in gold bouillon than have to remember that night more than I can help."

My brother Joe was born soon after. Luckily, he looked just like Mama, and I was young enough to still take a chance on loving him—actually loving him. The fact that there's some of Wallace in my brother just makes his steady good nature that much more a miracle. We all adored Joe from the start. He was a big, strong baby—so big and strong that he walked before he crawled. He'd pull himself up along the edges of things and speed along on tiptoe. We had to watch him closely. He pulled Grandaddy's spittoon down on himself and broke a toe before he was a year old. To this day, when he walks he looks like he's about to break into a run. Just seeing Joe brings a smile to my lips.

Mama had a hard time birthing that big baby. Doctors then didn't always know what they were doing—not that they do now—and Mama ended up with her female organs hanging out. The only thing that eased the pain was a sitz bath, so Grandmama and I would fix her one at least once a day. She wore a truss for years and when I married Marcus, he paid for Mama to go to a surgeon, who sewed her insides back up where they should have been.

Seeing what had happened to Mama, I had my doubts about men and marriage and babies. But like a fool, I got myself in the family way and ended up jumping off the bridge. Just like every woman.

Marcus is a meat-and-mashed-potatoes kind of man, so I set to mashing. The phone rang. *About time, Marcus,* I thought. *Where the hell are you?* I gave my hands a quick wipe across the apron and answered, fit to chew him out. But it was only Babs Alderink.

She said, "Hi, Lucy. I'm calling to remind you about the Worship Board meeting Tuesday night."

Worship Board. I'm telling you. We used to call them committees. Now, they're boards. Some on the committee—not Babs, she's all right—are something else. They'll try every fad that comes along. I'm surprised we're not all wearing crystals. They've got to bring in flutes or guitars, when we have a perfectly fine organ we paid a pretty penny for. Well, at least they're there, in church. I don't get people who never darken the door. Don't try to tell me God's not important—most can't even swear without Him.

Then there's Pastor Cross. Now, Pastor Grange was comfortable, like an old shoe, but he could pitch some fire and brimstone. Cross wouldn't know brimstone if it set his hair on fire. Jesus the shepherd is well and good, but let's not forget Jesus the table turner. Oh, Cross is all right for a minister, I guess, but no matter what you say to him, he looks like butter wouldn't melt in his crack. And talk about a bleeding heart! He fills his sermons with teary lamentations about injustice in places we can't do anything about. All he accomplishes is that we all feel guilty and no one has a pleasant worship experience. It's no wonder churches in this country are in such bad shape.

I can't see bringing politics to the pulpit, or letting it all hang out. Marcus and I have always agreed on one thing completely—you've got to play your hand close to your chest. I make a practice of not telling anyone anything personal, or important. People are going to believe what they want, anyway.

"Thanks, Babs," I said. "I'll be there." I hung up and said out loud, "If I'm not in the clink, that is, locked up for murder."

I feel bad about it now, but that's what I said. Things weren't always like that between Marcus and me. They were good once—real good—which, considering life with Wallace, was sort of a surprise. If I do say so myself, I used to be a looker. I inherited Daddy's dark hair, with Mama's auburn tints, and I cut a nice-looking female figure. Not too little, not too much. Marcus said he noticed that about me, right off.

When we met, I was waitressing at the Bottomless Cup, and he was home for the summer from college up north. He came in one morning, early, as I was taking the order at a table by the door. He nodded—I noticed how his eyes flashed blue—then he moved to the counter, hitched his pant legs up, placed the flat of one hand on the stool and mounted it from behind.

Phoebe Dalkins was working the counter. She gave it a quick, wet swipe in front of where he'd sat down and said, "What can I get you?"

"You can get Red over there to bring me some sausage and biscuits, please, ma'am." The whole restaurant was listening.

"Red, hmmm? All right. Lucy, this one's yours—I'll get the fellows from the granary." She gave me a *watch-out-for-him* look as she passed.

I knew who he was. Everybody did. The Talbots own the farm equipment factory back home and are local royalty. Marcus acted like someone used to getting what he wanted, but I gave him a run.

"First of all, I'm Lucy, not Red. My hair is brown."

"It's red in the sun."

"Hadn't noticed any sun in here."

"You didn't notice me, either, parked out front when you left yesterday. The door opened and you stepped out into the light, pulling pins. That hair was fiery, a billowing sun. Lord-ee, Miss Lucy. If I was ancient and an Egyptian, I'd have got down on my knees."

The granary guys took to snorting and sniggering.

"You want a shovel with those biscuits?" I said.

Marcus had it all, societally speaking, and damned if he wasn't a pretty boy to boot. Lust and practicality saw me coming a mile off. I was wanting to be caught. I thought I was doing the right thing. Marcus was handsome, he had a way that reminded me of Daddy, and like I said, I was in the family way. I'd gotten myself into something and my monthly was late. I was pretty sure I was pregnant but hadn't told a soul. A girl's a tad reluctant, when she's not sure who to blame. I was in the bad spot of needing to find baby a name. I looked the situation over from every side. It seemed to me we could all come out ahead. Marcus would have a wife in his bed—a decent-looking one. I'd have a husband's boots under mine. And the dear little problem would have her daddy and never know the difference.

I feel sorry for women who get sentimental about these things. A while back, our church had a Women's Convocation. A hundred-some ladies showed up. Toni Sprague-Heller was the speaker. She teaches at the college, social stuff, and Bugs Fletcher had asked her to talk about marriage. Toni has ideas that will give you whiplash. She's a feminist. Now, I'm amused by women who see the Devil everywhere, though I agree with some of what they're saying. After watching Mama and Wallace, I figured if a man laid a hand on me, I'd shoot his nuts off. Why all the anguish? And why get suicidal? I can't see making yourself penniless over some pie-in-the-sky principle.

Look at Toni, and you'll see a quiet redhead. Well, a quiet redhead in a funny pancake hat. Then she opens her mouth. I ask you, why a fancy word when a plain will do? And why a hundred words when ten are as good? Bugs got us off on a sidetrack, asking Toni what she thought about changing the words in old hymns—all those morons taking out the He's and His's. Toni said she didn't know, she didn't feel strongly, then she went on for a half hour about words having power. She said something about the way we talk being a mirror. I don't think a one of us really got it.

Toni's out to save the world—she's got this bumper sticker, ANOTHER DAY, ANOTHER DIFFERENCE—but at least she backs her talk with the goods. At the women's shelter she's right in the trenches. She told us there are people in her field who believe a day will come when no one will get married. That raised a few eyebrows. The idea is, we know that marriage doesn't work. People are figuring out they can live together, even have children, without signing on the dotted line or going through some ceremony.

And wasn't I born forty years too soon?

Well, sometimes your contract is clubs. Jan Doren brought up the news coverage on domestic violence since Nicole Simpson died. Toni said the attention is great—we need our eyes opened. After living with Mama and Wallace, I couldn't agree more. But she also said you've got to look at the whole story. Some researchers into that kind of thing, at it for twenty years, have found most families aren't violent. But in the ones that are, the women are just as likely to haul off on their partner. She even pointed out, and this tickled me, lesbians will take a whack at one another as often as normal people will.

Toni moved us into discussion groups afterwards, and, in ours, some pathetic views came out. Bugs had lost her husband, a year or so before, and was recently engaged. *Good God,* I thought when I heard about it. *The woman's a martyr.*

"Bugs," I said. "Get a cat. You can leave for a few days and they're fine."

"You don't know," she said. "You have Marcus. I miss having someone, someone who's there for me every day. The kids have their own families. I can't expect them to drop everything and take up the slack."

Bea Markowski's husband has advanced Alzheimer's. I watch her in church sometimes and don't know if I more pity or admire her. She rubs his back like they were the two of them there alone. She said, kind of hesitantly, like Bea does, "I love Art and wouldn't trade him for the world, but aren't you afraid you'll end up nursing an invalid and fighting with his kids?"

Toni was checking in with the groups, and she walked over just as Bugs said, "Frank's kids are wonderful. Besides, there's no guarantees in life. I could have died in childbirth, too, but I had babies anyway. Well, I guess that may be because I couldn't say no and they just came along." That got her a laugh, especially from Naomi Kinnunen, an old gal who had a litter every other year. The laugh encouraged Bugs, so she rambled on. "I'm hearing that what I eat these days could do me in, but I say grace and eat three square meals anyway. Since I've got to eat, or die—I eat. I want to be with Frank, and that means marriage, whatever it brings. None of this living together." Bugs turned to Rena Cross, sitting there with her mouth zipped up, like always. "What do you think, Rena? About marriage?"

Now, I don't know why everybody looks to the minister or his wife. It seems to me they might be the most naïve people in town. Rena Cross is a smooth one. She thought for a while, like she might say something a real person would say. Then she comes out with, "If I answered, I'd be spilling Cross family secrets. You wouldn't want that. Besides, Toni's the one to ask. She maybe knows me better than I know myself."

Toni spun on her heels. "Don't look at me!" We all looked at her anyway, so she signaled the whole group to give her their attention, then she said, "I've got to say this. Life brings all kinds of experiences. As you're talking here, don't compare yourselves." She set the groups to discussing again and turned back to us. "I'd guess Rena would rather be married than not." She smiled this rueful-looking smile and said, "Then there's me. I'm not so sure. You'd think someone who's spent years teaching Marriage and the Family could have pulled off her own marriage better than I did—oh! I just compared myself. . . . Don't tell the others."

We all laughed. If you ask me, the woman's on the outs with a pearl of a man, as good-natured as he is good-looking. He's always opened the door for me at church with a wink and a cheeky "And how's Mrs. T?" He's disappeared since their trouble, and I have to say I miss the impertinent thing. I wouldn't mind having thirty years back. I wouldn't waste it, like some women do. Of course, the ladies couldn't leave me out of it. Bea turned to me. "What about you, Lucy?"

I looked them all right in the eyes, paused, and said, "If something happened to Marcus, I'd never get married again." They all clucked and nodded—I'd said just the right thing, as usual. But where they took my words to mean I was that much in love, what I really meant was I'd be rid of him. And no, sir-ee, I wouldn't need to cozy up to some limp geezer to continue to live life in the manner I'm accustomed to. Money's the only thing that sets a woman free. The old feminists knew that—but try telling the new breed. It's not a hard-enough concept. There's not enough whining and blaming in it.

That's what I said. But that was another day. Now that it was getting on toward six, I was starting to get worried. When you're my age, plain old pissed-off-ness at your spouse isn't so easy to come by. Whether you like him or tolerate him, you're always thinking at the back of your mind, *Maybe something happened to him.*

Dinner was ready, if the old man would just show up. I was getting more and more concerned, and I went and stood at the window in the street-side sitting room. The Murphy kids across the way were raking huge piles of leaves by yard light and burrowing into them, the way kids will. Just watching, I could smell the loamy odor of leaves on the ground, could hear the *crunch crunch* sound they make. The wind was picking up, sucking the leaves as fast as the kids could rake.

Their mother stuck her head out. "Aaron, button your coat." The boy made a distracted attempt at buttoning with one hand and kept on raking with the other.

Kids. Our Joey was born seven months after we got married. I started seeing Marcus the day we met but put him off a couple weeks before giving in. You know what I mean. I didn't want to appear too anxious. A few weeks later, I told him I was pregnant. I've got to say, he never flinched. One thing about Marcus is he's never shirked duty. Before I could turn around, we were in front of the J.P., and in the fall I went north with him. The family bankrolled us without any trouble, and we've been here ever since.

Lucky thing, Joey came late rather than early. First babies being so unpredictable, the timing didn't seem that far off. Of course, it was perfectly obvious to anyone nosy enough to count that I'd fished without a license—but it wasn't obvious I'd fished with somebody else.

Joey is my one true happiness.

He looked enough like me to make up for the lack of Marcus in him. What he does have of Marcus's is his drive. He has a high-paying job as an arts administrator in Boston and a summer home on the Cape. Marcus and I take Amtrak out there every summer. It's a funny thing—I'm happy on the train. It was a train that took Daddy, but he did love them. He'd tell me about the rising and falling of the whistle, the way the landscape moved past—fast up close, slow farther away. It's sad. We have to drive to catch the train, there are only freight trains through here now. Getting rid of the old train system was the stupidest thing this country ever did.

Joey calls a couple times a week. He's so lucky in his friends—artist types, most of them. Writers, painters, musicians. And my favorite—actors. He fits with them, and that makes this mother happy. But I can't get him to settle down. "Oh, Ma!" he groans, when I prod him. "Leave it alone. I'm very happy the way things are." He smiles Daddy's smile and makes pudding out of my heart. Now, I know wedded bliss is an old wives' tale. But the arrangement does have its benefits, and it bothers me that Joey's getting to an age where no one's going to want him. If he would just meet someone and settle down, I'd feel I've done my job.

Marcus doted on him from the moment he was born. They were fishing, playing ball, and going on camping trips almost before Joey was out of diapers. Our photo albums from that period are one long series of snapshots of the two of them. Marcus holding Joey as if he was made of porcelain, at a week old. Marcus with Joey on his lap, holding two fluffballs, the first of many kittens. Marcus standing alongside Joey at the circus pony ride, keeping him upright when his legs were too short for the saddle. Father and son striking identical, hand-in-the-pocket poses on either side of a long stringer of bluegills and perch.

We didn't worry at first that there weren't other babies coming. But by Joey's third birthday, we were starting to wonder, and by the time he was six, we were concerned. No one talked about such things, the way they do now—unless it was behind your back. Babies were acts of God, and so was the lack of them. But the Talbots have never been folks to take difficulties laying down, so Marcus swallowed his pride and asked old Doc Mortenson about it.

No one in a small town knew much back then about why people couldn't have babies, even the doctors. Doc referred us to a Dr. Sylvester down at the U. We made the long trip one bright spring morning. It was the last bright morning we ever spent together.

*M*arcus had his semen checked. Believe it or not, it was all they could do. When we went back in for the results, Dr. Sylvester cleared his throat. He said, careful as a kitten on tinfoil, "You have very few sperm, Mr. Talbot. Almost none at all."

Marcus turned sort of blue, didn't move a hair.

I felt myself go pale.

Dr. Sylvester blundered on, "It's a hard blow, I know—the sort of report I regret having to give a couple. I can't say if there are problems with Mrs. Talbot, but the low sperm level alone makes pregnancy unlikely. The bad news is there's nothing to be done about it. Frankly," he said, as if he'd never heard of goings-on behind the woodpile, "it's remarkable you have your son. You ought to be thankful for him."

Gentle as he was trying to be, the doctor's words hit me like a house wall falling. I knew what he was saying, even if he didn't. My vision started to blur, and I got this hot, dizzy feeling. I had visions of Wallace stumble-dancing around the backyard, firing his gun. A feeling of panic hit me, and waves of stabbing contractions started rolling through my lower body. It took me a second to recognize what was happening. I couldn't believe it. Fully clothed in the doctor's office, I was having a climax—without anyone laying a hand on me. A while back, I read in a ladies' magazine at the hairdresser that what happens in our bodies when we're afraid is linked to what happens when we do the deed. My head was nodding so hard, over a mystery explained, that the receptionist came over and asked if I was all right.

Getting the word from Doctor Sylvester, I must have gone a bit green, because he said, "There now," and jumped up and got me a glass of water. I'd kept my secret for so long, I was sure

I was safe. But now here was this kindly doctor, smiling sympathetically and patting us on the shoulders, letting a wife-eating tiger out of the bag.

We didn't say a word about what Sylvester said until we were in the car, driving. Marcus is the kind who clams up when something's bothering him. I glanced sideways at him. "Marcus," I made myself say. He had both hands on the wheel, and his face was closed. "Honey. It's all right. I—I don't care. That we can't . . . have any more."

He kept his eyes on the road. When he answered, his voice was tight. "Listen. Luce. I don't want to discuss it, not ever. You understand? There's nothing we can do—so there's nothing to talk about." He glanced at me, turned those blue lights for just a second. "Is there?"

There wasn't. I kept my chin up but turned my eyes away, let my mind close around a circle of black-and-white cows huddled in a field.

That drive was the longest I ever took. I had a bad spell later on, but at that point I was too scared to feel sad. When we got home, Joey met us at the door. He was in his cowboy hat, footy pajamas, and holster. He jumped into Marcus's arms. "Twirl me, Daddy. Twirl me." Marcus did, then put him back down and looked him over like he was seeing him the first time.

"Were you a good little man for Julia? Of course you were. You're my Joey." Marcus hugged the boy so hard I thought my heart would give out. Joey didn't notice, but Marcus looked like he was going to cry. He didn't, of course. But from then on, I knew. Marcus knew that Joey wasn't his—and he knew I knew. We've had some barnburner fights in the years since, but Marcus never brought up that, and I didn't, either. I owed him that. I always thought it would be too much for him to hear me say it.

To Marcus's credit, he never took it out on Joey. It wasn't the boy's fault. But then, when it's come to Joey, Marcus has always been an easy mark. He had no call to learn the hard lessons about love I learned as a child. He threw himself into it with Joey, and even in a man, love for a child can be hard to break. It would be about as likely that Marcus would go out and pour gasoline all over his garden and drop a match in it as that he'd stop loving Joey.

He wasn't that hard on me, either. Marcus and I have lived by a code of obligation. Got a lot, give a lot. Speak a pledge, keep it. Especially one spoken before the Lord. Divorce was out of the question, but Marcus did pull away, and I let him. It was easier for both of us. Easier to pretend our marriage had just bottomed out over the years, the way marriages naturally do. The important thing was, we were civilized. We based our life together after that around other things.

Marcus never touched me again, not once in all these years. Once I got used to the idea, not having marital relations wasn't as hard as you'd think. That part of me was a garment I took off, folded, and tucked into a drawer. The only trouble I had was when I reached my change and I let some fool doctor talk me into hormone shots. They had me so horny Marcus started looking dreamy. I went back to the clinic and said, "I'm not having any more of those infernal things. Take 'em yourself, if you're so interested."

The situation between Marcus and me suited me. After what had happened to Mama when Joe was born, I didn't mind not having to worry something like it would happen to me. As for Marcus's needs, I don't know if, or where, he went for them. He probably did, but as long as he didn't embarrass Joey or me, I left it his business. We kept up appearances. As long as Joey was at home, we continued to sleep in one bed, an invisible line down the center. But when Joey went East to boarding school, Marcus and I moved into a bigger house and started sleeping in separate rooms.

By now, that old story is so much water under the bridge. I don't know why it came back to me today. As I waited, the clock

I gave Marcus for our twenty-fifth struck six, and I turned away from the window. "The man can drive me crazy," I said out loud. I don't mind talking to myself. I know it's just a way of sorting things out. The feeling had been growing that something wasn't right. I couldn't exactly identify it, but something kept nagging at me.

I hate not being able to do anything, so I checked the foyer closet. The coat Marcus wore to work was on its hanger, neat as a pin—he's finicky about the condition of his clothes. But one of his casual jackets was missing, so I knew he'd been here and gone out again. I started looking around the house, and found his new Italian wallet and money clip on the desk in the den. That struck me as real strange. Marcus never goes anywhere without carrying a lot of cash.

The alarm bells started going off. I threw on a coat and a pair of Marcus's house slippers and went out to the garage. His car was there, but no sign of him. Things were starting to get eerie. Something told me to check the yard. I grabbed a flashlight off the workbench and turned the backyard light on.

"Marcus?" There was no answer.

I figured maybe he was at the woodpile. Marcus loves his woodpile. He loves wood. He spends hours splitting and stacking it, in perfectly straight rows, and he's dragged every man he knows out to look at it. "There's wood enough out here to heat a house for three winters," he says.

"Ain't it something?" they'll say.

Or, "Nobody plans that far ahead anymore."

"Yeah," Marcus will agree. "And I split every chunk of it myself."

They all shake their heads and act like he deserves a medal. Never mind we heat with gas.

I passed the crab apple tree and the oak grove, branches clacking in the wind, and skirted the remains of the garden. There I got the shock of my life. I'd been cursing the man for almost an hour, and the whole time he was laying in the yard, his body wedged cock-eyed between his beloved chopping block and woodpile. The ax was on the ground, nowhere near him. No blood. Sticks of kindling everywhere.

"Jesus," I said.

At first, I thought there was hope. But when I dropped to my knees and really looked at him, I knew he was gone. His skin was ashen, one eye was open, the other one closed. I reached for his hand—actually, it was like I was standing behind myself and saw myself reach for it. The fingers were very cold. *Sweet Jesus,* I thought. I couldn't believe it. Marcus never got sick. I let his hand drop and stumbled back to the house.

There were signs everywhere, if only I'd seen them. The screen was moved to the side of the fireplace. The wood caddy was missing from its spot. The kitchen door had been unlocked. But I was so intent on getting to the theatre, I walked around blind.

My mind couldn't decide what to do with itself. The last thing I expected when I got up this morning was I'd be widowed by nightfall. I was starting to feel some real strange emotions. I thought, *Okay, Lucy. You've got to call someone. You've got to call Joey.* I'd been walking around in a daze, but the thought of telling Joey about his father made my heart lurch. I didn't know how I was going to make that call.

I dialed 911. The dispatcher said she'd send an officer and an ambulance.

"He's dead. An ambulance isn't going to do any good."

"Mrs. Talbot, it's standard procedure. Are you all right there alone?"

"Of course I'm all right. The only other person here is dead." The woman just didn't seem to be grasping the situation.

"I understand that, ma'am. Would you like me to stay on the line with you until the officer arrives?"

I let her know I was just fine and hung up. Then I regretted it. The house was so big, so quiet. I went to wait by the front door and noticed every sound. Half-forgotten family stories came whispering back.

Some of us have been known to die and stick around. When Grandpa Matusek passed, he kept showing up for months. Grandma would hear the bedsprings in his room squeak as if he'd stepped out of bed, then she'd hear footsteps. She'd go up and look, but no one would be there. Other times, she'd hear him talking upstairs. She'd peek up the stairwell, and he'd be sitting on the bed carrying on a conversation with someone or something. To her, he never said one word. She was so unnerved, she thought for a while she'd have to move out. But then his visits stopped.

Then there's the case of Great Aunt Flo. After her death, her house was sold outside the family, and for a while strange things happened. No one ever saw Aunt Florence herself, but the new owners confided to my cousin Althea that they'd be awakened at night by the light in their room turning on, and the sound of tables and chairs moving around downstairs. When they'd get up to check, nothing was moved. But every light in the house was on, from the basement to the attic. Or they'd come home and find one leaf clipped from every potted plant. "The leaves are placed carefully beside the pots," they said, like they really didn't think Althea would believe it. "Straight cuts, not like some insect bit them off."

The whole thing perplexed us. Maiming plants wasn't like Aunt Flo. She'd been a well-mannered person. Now, California can keep all that New Age nonsense . . . but I know there's things going on we don't control. I figured it would be just my luck for Marcus to decide to hang around.

I heard the ambulance coming long before it showed up, and then it did, and then the police car. I took them out back. I knew from the slow way the paramedics did things, I was right. Marcus was gone. The woman sat back on her heels, glanced at her partner, and shook her head. He looked up at me and said,

"Sorry, Mrs. Talbot. . . . Has your husband had a history of health problems?"

"No. Nothing."

The police officer got in on it. "There will have to be an autopsy, ma'am. In cases of unexpected death, like this, the coroner gets involved." He took me by the elbow. "Would you like to go inside, where it's warm? It may be a while before this is wrapped up."

I guess I nodded, because the next thing I knew, I was being guided up to the house. Marcus and I never leave loose ends. We prearranged everything at Gunderson's. I expected, when one of us dropped, Charlie Gunderson would back his white hearse up to the door and take care of things. It would be simple and clean. I couldn't have been more wrong.

"Anyone you'd like to call, Mrs. Talbot?" The officer sat me by the kitchen phone and pushed it at me like I ought to use it. He smiled encouragingly and gestured toward it again. His eyes drifted over to the table that Lorna left so beautifully set, and he shook his head. Half to make him feel better, I picked up the phone and hit "0" for the parsonage.

It seemed like the thing to do. Cross picked up after a number of rings, with his usual elevator-boy tone. Despite myself, I almost cracked. I had a hard time finding my voice. But then I pulled out of it and gave him the short version of the story. It was the least I could do, have him come for Marcus. He said he'd be right over.

I don't know why, but as I waited, I started to get mad. The thought went through my mind, *It's just like Marcus, to up and die.* He was probably howling down in the game room over the trouble he was causing, ready to sling his knapsack over his shoulder and head for the tracks. Now I wouldn't be able to make it to opening night, and Claire was counting on it. She's been talking about the play for weeks. I kept seeing her big green eyes, how happy she was when she said, "Hug me for luck?"

Then I started to get mad that Marcus was laying out in the yard. It was freezing out there and getting darker. I kept seeing him the way he was the day we met. He walked into the Bottomless like he owned the place. His clothes and shoes were the finest you could buy. His back was ramrod straight, yet he moved like a lynx. One flash of those blue eyes, and the rest was fate.

Just because we've had hard times doesn't mean I won't do right by him. It's only human decency. The fact that a person's dead doesn't mean he should be treated like a block of wood. The world gets you, coming and going. Who'd have guessed you have to stand in line even when you're dead? After I was sitting there awhile, I realized how insulting the whole thing was. The way it was being handled, you'd think I poisoned him or something.

I don't know how it happened.

I heard the oven click and remembered the food keeping warm in it. All of a sudden, those damn potatoes popped into my mind and my eyes flipped over in my head and took a look inside. Damned if there wasn't a six-year-old in there, crying and shaking like a leaf on the back porch swing. I heard her thoughts and felt her quaking like she was connected to me at the end of a long tunnel.

That's when Cross arrived. The front doorbell rang, and when I opened it, he was standing there looking like Mama and Daddy rolled into one. His lips pressed together. He shook his head. "Oh, Lucy," he said. All he did was say my name, and Lady Luna was gone. He held his arms out—and I'll be damned, I stepped right into them. I started to shudder.

"There, there," Cross said, patting my back. "There, there now, Lucy. Even the best of scrappers needs to let it out, once in a while."

The damn man knew just the thing to say.

I bawled like a baby.

Mirrored in the Sky

It was full dark now. The kids at the convenience store had gone. Some, home to their families. Others, to private rendezvous. Leaves from the tall maple tree at the edge of the parking lot had blown up against the door. Their colors, the blood tones and sun tones, were muted in the artificial light. When someone opened the door, the leaves scattered with a grating sound.

At the Larkspur Theatre, halfway up the long hill from the lake to the bluff, the curtain was about to rise. Paired headlights ascended and descended the hill and waited patiently to enter the lot. It was cold enough now that smoke blew away from the tailpipes. But one set of lights kept straight on—it went down the hill and did not turn. It was the ambulance, no lights or siren now. Above the hill, on a mirrored hill in the sky, the pelican flew low, then high.

Inside the theatre, the cast was coiffed and garbed. They waited. Ticket takers worked the doors. The theatregoers were in high spirits. They laughed and talked, then took their seats and leafed through programs. Some were finely dressed, others in jeans. All were unaware of the stage manager running his track—something needed to be handled in the lobby, the box office, the dressing rooms. There was always something, backstage. As he ran, he kept one eye on his watch—everything was ready.

Now the magic would start.

Claire Collier

*W*hen you're a child, you're afraid of the dark. But when you grow up, you love it. No—you love the almost dark. Even a small light, in the distance, keeps fear away. So you can taste the dark. Breathe it. Wrap it around you like a robe and relax into it. Without dark, you wouldn't know light.

Backstage was dark—and electric.

Ten minutes earlier, the whole cast had been telling jokes and had gotten the lightning giggles. But we were so close to curtain now, we were dark. In the last minutes, you're wondering how you got yourself into this. Jack and Patrice had to go on first—they were deep in their own worlds. Jack was off in a corner doing stress-relieving exercises. The sleeves of his smoking jacket billowed in the blue light as he swung them through butterfly circles. Trice was walking back and forth and bouncing up and down on three-inch heels, shaking her fear out her fingertips.

I've never been able to decide if it's harder to open the action, or wait. The character I'm playing now doesn't make an appearance until scene four. So I filled the time and my mind repeating my pre-curtain prayer. *Jesus Christ, Son of God, have mercy on me, a poor sinner.*

It seems strange, maybe, to say those words backstage of a play, especially one called *Murder, Et Cetera.* But it's always worked for me. It calms me down. The theatre is a place of superstition. Everyone has their own habits and rituals. Gordy wears the same shabby sneakers to Call—I'd guess they're vintage 1970. "There's always duct tape," he says. "I'll wear these until the soles fall off." His girlfriend, Vera, has a different vibe going on. I use that word because it's so them. Vera keeps a statue of the Buddha on her dressing table and rubs its belly before going backstage.

Some traditions you'll find everywhere.

You're never supposed to say the name *Macbeth* inside a theatre. If you've got to say it, you say *the Scottish play.* If you forget and say the forbidden word, you have to spit, swear, and go outside and turn around three times. Who knows where the spitting and swearing came from. But the magic number three and the circles are understandable. You're not to whistle in the dressing room, and you can never say "good luck." You have to wish broken limbs on one another, instead.

Phil bolted through in his stage-manager frenzy. His shirt was white and glowing in the dim light.

"Two minutes to places," he whispered. "Break a leg, everyone. Two minutes."

We all gathered and hugged and whispered. "Break a leg. Break a leg. Good show. Good show, Claire." Then we waited. We're not professionals. But we do a good job. Trice and Jack were so focused, the whole backstage seemed to collapse into them.

Finally, Phil uttered the crucial word.

"Places."

No backing out now.

The house lights pulsed down to black—onstage, they went up to blue. Jack made his way out and struck a suspicious-looking pose at the top of the staircase. Trice arranged herself elegantly in the armchair by the fireplace, her back to him. When the lights came up, we were in a different world. The Jack Berry we knew—the wild man in mirrored Vuarnets and three-season Bermuda shorts—had been replaced by scheming Biff Summers. And Patrice Bukowski, small-town mother of three, didn't even look like herself. She was the beautiful and entitled Mariah Mayweather. Rehearsals were such a hoot, I'd expected opening to be riotous and fun. But here it was, and my spirits were lower than low. No one I'd hoped to be there had come.

I peeked out at the audience again. There was no mistake. Lucy's and Marcus's seats at front row center were big, bright, and empty. I didn't understand it. They were an institution at opening night. When I left the store, Lucy said, "We'll be there, hon—have we ever missed?" I've worked for her nearly five years and never knew her to make a promise she didn't keep. What really disappointed me, though, was that nowhere in the audience did I see Richard Cross.

When I was young, everybody loved Claire. I was a perfect child, I never did anything wrong. But then I lost my innocence on a bathroom floor and turned wild. There was an unending cyclone in my chest, a cloudburst in my head—and since my divorce things have only gotten worse. I'll find my purse well chilled in the fridge, the milk going sour in a cupboard. Some days, I think I should just check in at the state hospital. Everything I once believed in lies like china shattered to a gift shop floor, and time is screwed up. I'm haunted by poltergeist twins. Wherever I go, they remind me where I've been. I'll be fine, minding my own business—then *wham*, I'm back in time, it's like I'm there again, where I don't want to be. My heart's racing, I can't breathe. My past and my present stagger around inside my head, drunks arm-in-arm, taunting me, pissing their way down an alley.

Tonight started on a bad note. On my way to the theatre, I nearly got taken out by an ambulance coming around a corner.

I pulled over quick, heart thumping. I'm raw nerves as it is, on opening night. I didn't need that.

And later—no Richard.

The whole time I was waiting for my cue, I kept thinking, *He didn't come.* I was being smacked by tsunamis of embarrassment. I was angry, angry with Richard and angry with myself. A minister, that kind of man, is the last I'd want. But Richard is . . . he's savvy, at the heart, and there's something about that. He's a man I would like to want. When I saw he hadn't come, I thought, *You're such a fool. What would you have done, if he'd shown up? Screw him,* I thought. *Screw all men. Who needs them?*

"Good for you, Claire."

I could almost hear Richard's voice, so low and reassuring. He would say it, and mean it. In my mind I looked up and saw his eyes, those deepest, darkest eyes. I began seeing him for counseling when I started attending his church after Paul and I separated. Actually, after Lucy dragged me to services. The first session, he listened, then said, "Why are you beating yourself up over this?"

God. As if a person had to ask.

We'd just finished the courtroom phase of the divorce, and I was a wreck. The day before, a woman in my book club had said, with me sitting right next to her, her perfect bad example, "Divorce is just too easy." Her tone was pointed, cruel. Inside me something bent in on itself. It gave the poltergeists an in. A voice cackled in my ear, *So what? So what if, the night before the hearing, you threw up and threw up? So what you had the shakes, you were shivering, you were emotionally numb? And so what, Baby Girl, your life sloughed down the toilet and you couldn't cry a drop?* I hadn't—haven't—been able to, in months.

Lucky Richard.

I kept going to his church because it felt right. The first time I attended a service with Lucy, as we entered the church we passed a collage of broken mirror shards. Lucy stopped and stared into it.

There we floated, in pieces.

"What's this?" she said. "There aren't enough mirrors in the world? You don't know about that. I envy you, Claire. I wish I was back in my twenties." Lucy blows me away sometimes. She said, "I say this only to you, dear—I have moments my body buzzes to be some guy's lollipop again. I used to be, you know. Then I pass a mirror or a window on the street, and I get this shock because some old thing who looks a lot like me walked though it. Then I realize it was me, and I feel like parking myself on the curb, to laugh maybe, or cry."

During the sermon, Richard's point was, we reflect Christ in the world. He said, "Are you thinking, 'Ridiculous, no way'?" He paused. "Now, I'm not going to bare my soul here, because I like my job." There were chuckles, guffaws. "Look inside you," he said. "What you see there, you'll see in here." He touched a hand to his chest. "If God can see fit to have something to do with this, God can do the same with you." He gestured to the entryway. "Look in the mirror as you leave. That's you, the crabbed hands and dirty feet of Jesus. Kind of a mess. But lean into it, see where it goes."

If crabbed hands and dirty feet are the ticket, I'm in the front row.

Divorce isn't easy—it's a terror. Paul, my ex, is Methodist so when we got married, I became Methodist, too. I was happy there. There ought to be a ceremony where a woman going through divorce kisses goodbye her husband's coworkers, half their friends, all his relatives if there are no kids involved, the credit card company—who will pull her card, but not his, on her worst day—and even their church if it was his church first. When we split, I couldn't just move to another pew. I left the congregation. Given how my head was, if not for Lucy I might have left church altogether.

In answer to Richard's question—why I was beating myself up—I said, "Because it's my fault."

"What makes you say that?"

"It must be. Paul didn't even want the divorce."

"That's not unusual. Why did you want it?"

Richard brings out the deuce in me. I could have told him, for one, that Paul's eyes once flooded at the sight of a toddler being guided up a steep stairwell by his mother. I had come up quietly. But so private was his moment, I stepped back. He hadn't known I'd seen. We'd been trying—both of us wanted a baby, more than we wanted to breathe—but every month, nothing. The doctors couldn't say why. I could have told Richard, but didn't. I said, "I don't know why I wanted it. If I knew that, maybe we could have done something about it and I'd still be married."

Richard thought awhile. "Okay. I guess that's not somewhere you want to go." He brought his fingers together, tip to tip, thought some more, then unlinked them. "Let me try it this way. You're telling me the problems in the marriage were only your fault?"

He studied me without expression. But it was clear "yes" would be the wrong answer. I said nothing, shifted in my chair, crossed and uncrossed my legs. How do you tell someone that what you know, and what you feel, are two different things?

When I was a kid, eight, maybe, or nine, I found a baby robin in the yard. Its needy mouth kept opening and closing, opening and closing. I thought about fixing up a dryer-lint bed in a shoebox and trying to raise it myself. But I decided to put it back into the nest. I had to climb the tree to do it, and I went in to dinner feeling elated and heroic.

When I was excused from the table, I ran back out to check on it and found its little body lifeless against the trunk of the tree. I just knelt there, looking at it.

My dad came out to see what I was doing.

"Too bad," he said. "You touched it. Makes the mother bird reject it."

I don't know if it's even true—a mama bird pushing its baby from the nest. If it is, I didn't cause it on purpose. I know that.

But I feel like I did.

When I didn't answer—Richard's question about it being only my fault—he shook his head. "We don't have that problem at our house. We've got two people sure they're in the right."

You could have blown me over with a cocktail straw. I hadn't expected him to talk about his life, and it surprised me, about his wife—she's such a bland, starchy thing. In that moment, the man earned my regard. I knew I'd tell him everything.

I said, "You have problems?"

He laughed and leaned so far back I thought he would hit the frame of the large painting behind him. It was a folk art pelican. It's some kind of thing there, the pelican—Lucy wears a pelican charm that Marcus had made for her. The painting was simple and primitive, but the pelican seemed alive. It was the eyes. They were painted so they followed you. Whichever way you turned, they were there.

Richard's chair looked like it would tumble ass over crown. It was a pedestal-leg rocker, and every time he swung back, the spring squeaked. He said, "Surprised? Why? That we have problems, or that I'd tell you?"

"Both."

He rocked the chair forward. "I don't want you to think I'm talking from out of the clouds." He got this look on his face I can only call pained, and he said, "I was young once. Wasn't married, was having thoughts, here and there, maybe I'd be a pastor. Maybe. At the same time I was doing things I regret." He saw the skeptical look on my face and said, "You don't believe me?"

"What? You knocked over some kid's tuba at the bus stop?"

He laughed. "I see I've got my hands full, with you. No, there are things I truly regret, they should be regretted, and you know what? Some days I wish I could do them again." He pulled a pen out of a cup on his desk—the cup had a pelican on it, one on a nest—and started drumming on the desktop. "I use it, I use it every day to be a better pastor. It takes one to know one, you know? You really can't be there for someone you don't see." He dropped the pen back into the cup. "But we're not here to talk about me. Every couple's got problems, Claire. You must know that being married, or in any serious relationship, doesn't mean you're dead. You've got two people who are rowing together, and then, sometimes for no reason, there's a temptation to jump out of the boat."

I thought, *How curious.*

What happened with me wasn't a temptation. It was a desperation. I had to get out of the boat before . . . before I drowned in it. There was the baby I couldn't conceive—I suppose I should say *we*. When you want something, something you can't get, it makes you numb. But there was more. Once I was wearing a ring, I had become invisible. I was dead in the water, married to a guy whose yachts took all the trophies. I had become no one. By the end, Paul and I had nothing in common, we'd come more and more unglued. He had his eye on this little schnauzer at the animal shelter. He wanted it so bad, and he couldn't understand that I kept saying no.

It's hard to explain the things that happen at the end of a marriage. How the two of you behave, people who were once so in love. By the time we were coming up on our seventh anniversary, we'd gotten to where we couldn't talk without an argument. It seemed to come down on his side to my involvement in theatre. Somewhere along the line Paul had decided the theatre represented everything wrong in our marriage—that, if he could get rid of it, our problems would disappear.

One night, I'd had a really hard rehearsal. Austin Sloan was directing, and he can get pissy. He picked at everything I did. "Claire," he said, "you've dropped character six times in three minutes. I clocked you."

By the time he called it a night, I was ready to quit everything. Paul was already in bed when I came in, and as I undressed, he lit into me.

"What's the matter with those people?"

"What do you mean?"

"Don't they have lives, or homes? Nothing better to do than preen and strut around? Hit the bars? Leapfrog from bed to bed?"

"I wasn't at a bar. I haven't done bars since we got married. You're being ridiculous. Gordy, preening? Trice, sleeping around? It'd be like Mother Teresa doing it."

"Yeah, well. Take O'Neill. Even a dunce can see the numbers add up. What's Mr. Smooth on now—wife number three, or live-in number six?"

I flipped my camisole up over my head and tossed it into the hamper. Paul was forever leaving the cover up, like it was now, and it bugged me. "Sounds," I said, "like the pot calling the kettle."

"That's another thing, Claire. You're always throwing my divorce in my face."

"Look," I said. I'd heard his bitching about my theatre friends enough to be sick of it. "Why don't you just say what's bothering you? It's not O'Neill. It's not who's screwing who in the all-star lineup. It's me. You can't stand that I do this thing just for myself. With girls in your classes, it's 'You can do anything.' But the ones you marry? Get off it, Paul. I've had enough trouble in my life."

He rocketed out of bed and grabbed for his pants. "Good, Claire. That's real good. Fall back on 'Life's done me wrong.' Always works, doesn't it? Well, not this time, sweets. Where do you get off? You're not the only one who's been hurt."

He had his pants on and was reaching for his shoes, and he shot me an ugly glance. "Doing theatre is fine, but you have to be in every production. It's some kind of sickness with you. Go, go—see Claire go. You keep telling me you've put your past behind you. Christ, I don't see it. I don't think you want to have a baby. If you did, you'd have to sit still. You'd have to look at yourself."

It was a poison dart. I knew where it was coming from, but he had no idea, no right. "Don't psychoanalyze me," I said. "You're no shrink."

"You ought to know, you've seen enough of them." He gave me a look that was pure contempt and went out the door. Halfway down the hall, he threw over his shoulder, "I'll be at my folks'—if you're interested."

That was how our last arguments tended to go. Nothing was talked out. He'd leave, or I'd shut down. We were out of sync, completely. I don't hate Paul. I love him still. I know that's confusing. I could see he was wounded by what was happening with us, that it made him hold tighter. But I couldn't help him. It terrified me—but the last year, all I could think about was untangling us. It was like a disease in the brain, a fever, a tic. An endless washing and rewashing of hands.

When I got to feeling I had to tell somebody, I chose Lucy. I sat her down one afternoon when my shift ended. I said, "Lucy. I can't go home." I told her how heavy I was. I said I couldn't breathe.

She said, "Come to our place for dinner."

Lucy's a woman who says whatever's on her mind. While the lasagna was baking, we were in the great room. Marcus was there, too, and Lucy was playing mother hen. Honestly, she clucked. She said, "I can't say I'm surprised, Claire—we've noticed you taking on water. But, hon, think about what you're doing. I'm sticking my nose in here, but—why? Why would you leave? Is it . . . because you don't have any babies? Is that it? Is Paul . . . you know . . . refusing?"

"L-u-u-ucy."

"Well. There are men who want you knocked up every day of your life, and there are men who don't want to be bothered. Both boil my blood pressure. Some people just don't know what's good for them." She got this conspiratorial look on her face. "Some people," she said, "you have to help along a little. What're you using? The Pill?"

Across the room, Marcus folded his newspaper, got up from his chair, and said, "Excuse me, ladies. I think I'll start a fire."

"Good idea," Lucy said. "It is a bit chilly. When you come back, bring my afghan. It's in the den. And bring Claire a sweater, please. There's one in the foyer closet."

As he went by, I grabbed his sleeve. "Thank you, Marcus."

"No thanks needed, dear."

Once he was gone, Lucy said, "Well? Are you using the Pill?"

Lucy's like a grandmother to me, an outrageous grandmother. But I can see why when some people see her, they duck. She'll worry a subject to death—and you always end up feeling there's something you ought to be doing.

"Not the Pill," I said.

"What then?"

I felt my face flush. It was like being a teenager and having your brother, or your science teacher, who's your secret crush, bring up sex.

"Lord Almighty," Lucy said. She grabbed my knee and shook it. "Look at you, blushing like a bride—though I guess that blushing bride stuff is mostly hogwash these days. Get some spit in you. You're past time. You're married, aren't you? Well, if your man won't provide you the baby you've got coming, just take it. The Good Book says the Lord's on your side, when it comes to marrying and multiplying. Don't shake your head at me. He didn't say, 'Wear a bag and have fun.' Did He? No. And if the father-to-be squawks about what he promised when he said he did, there will be time later to put his suitcase on the porch. Packed. That usually brings them around." She mock-shook her finger at me. "If that man of yours is watching to make sure you put your rubber cookie in, you just smile at him, have a pee afterwards, and take the damn thing out. I have friends that's worked for."

I stared at her. Sometimes the things Lucy says don't quite square with her station in life. I could see her in some seedy dive, strutting it in a boa and high heels, tucking bills into her cleavage. She's got room in there for quite a few.

"I couldn't do that," I said. "It . . . it wouldn't be right."

As if I could be that lucky. The poltergeist twins were listening in. One of them leaned into my ear and whispered something he'd pulled from way back in my memory. *Lucky, Claire. You're a very lucky young lady.*

I ignored him. I said, again, "I couldn't, Lucy—even if it was the problem. But it's not. Really. It's not."

She looked at me like I was dense, or a liar. "Claire, you're a beautiful woman. But you've got a brain in your head. Anytime there's no babies, there's a problem. Don't you see that?"

My mind stopped in its tracks. I pictured Paul holding his infant niece—smiling at her, bouncing her on his knee. It made my heart ache. "We could adopt," he said, wiping dribble off the baby's chin. "Maybe look into the in vitro thing?"

Lucy Talbot. Pinball Wizard. She'd delivered a direct hit. The board came to life. Lights flashed, bells binged, numerals spun. How could a person come across the hidden room just

by stumbling down the corridors? I have this image in my head—
me, with a protruding abdomen and rolling step. Me, cranky
and touchier than usual. Me, happy for morning sickness, de-
lighted over swollen legs. I'm twenty-seven. There was a time I
thought I'd have wrapped up having kids by twenty-seven.

"Don't press," I said. "Please. I'm doing what I have to. I
promise."

She saw I wasn't going home and offered me a bed. I knew
she would. "For a few days," she said—like she might really care
if I overstayed my welcome.

Dear Marcus was unsurprised and totally gracious. I guess
a person would get used to things living with Lucy. As he tended
the fire, rearranging logs, blowing into them, he said, "Lucy and
I were raised on wood smoke. I wouldn't make it through a day
without it. Warm weather, we grill out. There's nothing like
steak cooked over an applewood fire. Cool weather, it's the fireplace." He put the screen into place, dusted his hands off one
against the other. The flames rose up suddenly, the wood
snapped. "Look at it. Isn't it beautiful? And listen to that wind
in the flue. We get a lot of wind up here on the hill. It's why we
bought here. Now—drinks." He turned to me, taking out an
imaginary pad, and stood awaiting my order. "What'll you have,
Claire? We've got everything."

"A Manhattan," I said.

I'd never had one in my life, and it seemed like something
to try. When I'd finished the first, while Marcus was mixing the
second, I excused myself, took a deep breath, and called Paul.
He wasn't happy. But there wasn't much he could do. I said,
trying to sound firm, not vague, "Lucy needed me. Have lunch
with me tomorrow. I'll meet you. Mariani's, 12:30."

He agreed, though not enthusiastically. I knew it was the
best plan. I'd tell him where he couldn't throw a fit. I spent the
night rehearsing the script—what I'd say, what he'd say back. I

felt as small as a baby in Lucy's nightgown and big sleigh bed. Around four, I slept a little.

Over lunch, I told him, "I'm not coming home."

He didn't believe it. He said, "What do you plan to do?" When I said, "Work, take some classes, and next year, I hope, grad school in acting," he snorted. It wasn't the most charitable response, or the most reasoned. The way I did it had pulled the room out from under him. But I couldn't have done it any other way. Facing him and saying those words took everything out of me. Paul knew that about me—how hard it is for me to stick to decisions. The things I can't predict or control rear up, with teeth, and I crumble. Even as I backed the car out of the parking spot when we were leaving, he stood there with a skeptical look in his eyes.

I had to steel myself. I rolled the window down. "Find somebody else," I said. "Have the life you want."

Lucy was a godsend. The next afternoon, I told her I needed to pick up a few things and asked if she'd drive to the house with me. "Happy to," she said. "I'll run interference."

It was good she'd come, because just as we were leaving, Paul showed up. Poor guy. He wasn't ready for Lucy. Her ears went back, her lips thinned, she fixed him with unblinking eye. "Collier," she said, "if you even think of bullying this poor child, I'll call the cops."

I can't say Paul ever bullied me. In fact, if anything, he took too much care. But I was glad to have reinforcements with me, just the same. All's fair, you know, in love, in war.

After Richard made his boat-jumping comment, I said, "I want you to know—other people weren't a problem with Paul and me. There was no one. It was just . . . us."

"Okay. That's a start. You used the plural pronoun. Us. Both of you, in your own ways responsible—I don't like the word 'blame.' Some of us have a way of wreaking havoc very passively. It makes us look good in our own heads, but the result is the same."

The thing I most love about Richard is he talks to you like you're a human being and he is, too. He doesn't drone at you, like some counselors I've seen. I like that. I like that he's open and careful at the same time, how he's serious but then he'll laugh at himself. His eyes are so dark, but they light up. I love to watch him speak—his whole body becomes an expression of what he's saying.

I hadn't been exactly forthcoming with Richard. There'd been no other man when Paul and I broke up—that's true. But by the time I began talking to Richard, there was. I had a sound in my head like a too-tight guitar string. It needed release, and one night after rehearsal the man offered it. After that night, I'd lie in my wasteland of a bed and remember his hand cupped to my breast. I'd taste and feel his lips. It was torture, it was good. I was a blackbird riding a wind-flung branch, wings spread, wanting more.

But—he had a wife.

She hovered at the back of my mind, unsuspecting, grotesque, until one night in a dream I got rid of her. I shoved her against a concrete wall and mashed her head into it. I pushed with all my might, held her by the hair and ground her face into the wall with all my will. Pulp ran down the wall.

Even in the dream, the coldness of my desire, how venomous it was, shocked me. But . . . what's done is done. I ran my hands down my hips, to cleanse them, and then I turned from the wall. My lover was beside me, and he took me in his arms.

"Now we can be together," I breathed.

He said nothing. We sank into a soft, enveloping chair and began pulling one another out of our clothes. A button was an

ecstasy—a buckle, an explosion. I climbed into his lap, knees
bent, head bowed, and I rode him. His breath was hot waves in
my ear, his hands were seared to my hips. I was out of my head
for it . . .

So out of it—I broke it off the next day.

You'd think I'd know how to feel about the divorce. After all, I
was the one who ended it. It's not like I got dumped for somebody. And as I told Richard, it's not like I left Paul for somebody. I'd spent my young life searching for the perfect love, the
perfect lover. I tried guys out, one after another, tried them on,
looking for that fit. It was a shock, after I'd been married awhile,
to realize I'd tied myself to someone imperfect. Worse, that I
was a good deal less than perfect myself.

I have mixed-up feelings about the marriage. The whole
time it was nickel-and-diming us to death, I had this impression
doors were opening and closing. I kept walking through them
like a headstrong steer going to slaughter. By the time I decided
to leave, it was the only decision possible. I somehow voluntarily
became a divorcée against my will. Once I'd decided on the guy,
it was forever. I never wanted to get a divorce, I would never
agree to one. Life sure upends a person. In a way—I know this
sounds strange—the whole scenario was out of my hands, like
some big dark angel was pulling the strings. I can't explain it.
You can't know until you've been there. But I do know this:
People have no right to be judgmental like they are, when they
find out.

I've changed since Paul and I met. I was so naïve I can't help
but laugh about it myself. My head was somewhere else. Not
that I knew it, though. I moved to town right after high school,
with my life plotted out. I was starting over, no one had ever
seen my picture or read a word about me. I figured I'd get a
med-tech degree and take care of myself.

It was one of my lamer ideas, and Paul didn't mind telling me. He was my advisor my first semester of college, though I didn't meet him until late term when we registered for spring semester. The way my life's gone, I should have been more cautious. About men. But I met Paul and began dreaming up reasons to drop by. When we got together eventually, he said it had been obvious I had a crush on him.

Obvious was right. One day I presented him with an apple-shaped candle in cellophane. A golden apple, gold cellophane. Then I emptied my book bag all over his floor. Paul sprang out of his chair to help me pick everything up. On my way out, I backed into the doorpost. I'd planned the dropped books, but not the door. I walked away euphoric and feeling like a klutz.

Paul kept his distance. He was professional, even blunt.

"Claire," he said, when I'd been coming around awhile, "doesn't it worry you that you can't stand the sight of blood?" He knew I'd failed the chemistry midterm but didn't bring it up.

I shrugged. "I wouldn't be touching it. Would I?"

Paul calls the shrug the freshman salute. He's always bemoaning the clueless first-year look. Things went terribly in chem. After months of pathetic lab work, I clawed my way to a D on the final. As I looked at the big, fat F posted on the professor's door, I saw an imaginary beaker puff its chest, point to the exit, and yell, "Out, out!" I knew I'd be an ex-science major when the new semester started. Better to face reality sooner than later, I suppose. I'd decided on medical technology only because it would give me an income and security. Awful reasons for doing anything long-term.

Theatre was where I needed to be.

I had my first inkling in fourth grade Sunday school. Mortified at being taller than most of the boys, I couldn't believe it when the teachers told me I'd be playing a Wise Man in the Christmas program. I found my parents in the narthex and, after a long, melodramatic moan, said, "I have to be a Wise Man—"

"Not now, Claire," Dad said. My parents are the introverted, unassuming type—a potent mix of Scandinavian and Minnesota Nice. They do their complaining behind closed doors, or if they're really unhappy, vote with their feet.

I nursed my distress through the coffee hour. The second we were out the door, I picked it back up. "I'm already eight feet tall, and they're going to make me wear a turban!"

"A turban?" my brother said and started to laugh.

"Collin," Mom warned. "Drop it."

Collin did, but I didn't. While Mom was making lunch, I followed her around, complaining.

"Honey," she finally said. "You're going to be tall. Accept it. You've got tall parents. Someday you'll be happy about it."

"I'll never be happy about it."

"Claire. The boys won't stay short forever. Someday they'll grow, more than you. Wait and see—you'll be just right, even in a turban. Now, am I supposed to be making this costume?"

My first taste of true theatre came a few years later in public school. I looked at the audition announcement for a musical and debated. Should I? Shouldn't I? In the end, I tried out. I knew I'd get a part. Then of course was astonished when I did. I got cast as the female lead. Backstage, I listened to the audience before the show. It was alive. It rustled, it murmured. I breathed in the smells of fresh-sawed wood and paint and the hot odor of the lights. I wondered what it would be like to pass out under them. But I didn't pass out, I didn't even come close.

I love the stage.

With that spotlight in my eyes, I'm changed. I can do whatever the script says. I can be a knife. Then I can pierce like an arrow, or resist like a rock. It doesn't matter that the real Claire cries at the drop of a hankie, or at least she used to, that she's run through by glances and remarks others just blow off.

I had a solo scene. I sang and danced and had the planet in my palms. I was so powerful. Maybe it was the red skirt and crinoline, or the makeup that gave me incredibly large eyes. Maybe it was the ponytail that swung like a blade every time I turned. It was a delicious shock to discover that, just by being a different me, I could bring the house down.

But when the makeup came off and my hair came down, a demon perched on my shoulder. *Are you crazy?* it whispered. *Calling attention to yourself? What if you forgot a line, and everyone looked at you? What if you fell? Or did a piss-poor job?* After I'd let it nag me for a while, I couldn't believe I'd done such a dangerous thing. I swore off future auditions.

I applied myself at school. I kept my nose clean.

It was no use. Sophomore year, something happened, something so bad I still don't like to talk about it. It flattened me for a while. But when I got back up, I knew what I wanted and when I wanted it. Nothing was going to interfere with my life ever again.

*W*ho'd have guessed that a simple line on my spring registration form—"Academic Advisor: Paul Collier"—would prove so fateful? I had decided I'd better check in with Dr. Collier and had a late afternoon appointment with him in his office in the biology department, second floor of Burnham Hall. Worried that I wouldn't find it on time, I got there early. Three students were already waiting outside his open office door. The four of us sprawled bored and impatient on the marble floor, listening to him talk. He went on and on in his deep voice about degree requirements and closed courses. We eyed each other nervously. Were we about to get bad news from some grizzled old prof?

At last, it was my turn. The girl ahead of me came out wearing a look of exasperation. Though it was almost winter, she was in Birkenstocks, with the addition of wool socks. She pushed her black-framed glasses up and lifted her bag to her shoulder. It was tie-dyed, every shade of pastel. I took in her dated look and thought, *What year does she think this is?* She was oblivious to my poisonous thoughts. She said, "I only got one of the courses I wanted. The rest were closed. Good luck. You're going to need it." There were never more oracular words. The Prophetess of Burnham stumped off down the corridor.

Paul stuck his head out.

The sight of him jolted me. He didn't look the way he sounded—he looked young. Not as young as me, but clearly not yet thirty. He had coffee-colored hair in a Beatle cut, and a trim mustache. He said, "I thought there was one more. You must be Claire."

I stood up, awkward suddenly. "I am." I was wearing clogs, which added to my height and leveled my eyes with his. But I found myself extending my neck to its longest and slenderest.

"Come on in." He chuckled. "Let's get you squared away before there aren't any classes left."

I didn't see the humor in the situation. I sat on a very hard chair across from his desk and looked around as he studied the schedule I wanted. His office was spare, cerebral. There were masks on the walls, scary and African in origin, and a large print of Edvard Munch's *The Cry* over his desk. What is it about a desk that makes people want to hang something odd over it? The print's jagged lines and haunted face kept drawing my eyes to it.

"Doesn't look too bad," Paul said. "We'll have to switch you to a different section for comp, though. Any objections to being in class by eight?"

"Uhhh. No."

I'd been avoiding eight o'clocks. But I didn't tell him that. In those days when someone pushed, I folded. Like a sheet. When Paul told me he hated even the idea of cream in coffee, I switched to drinking it black.

"No problem there, then," he said. "I don't know about Marriage and the Family. It's a popular class. Last word was it was close to full."

"Oh," I said. I was deflated. Marriage had been my only fun class.

Paul did a double-take. "Listen," he said. It was clear he felt bad, and I wondered how many times that day he'd had to say the same thing. Beyond the four I'd heard. "If we get this signed and to the registrar, you might be okay. I know it's a drag not to get the classes you want, or at least some of them." He reworked the form like he'd done it a million times, signed it with a scratch, and handed it to me. His lips turned up at the outside, in a quirky smile. "Scoot now," he said. "The race belongs to the quick."

I scooted, all right. I ran, one eye watching where I was going, the other staring at the way he'd signed his name. It was in dark blue ink, a signature forceful and bold. *Paul Collier.* The sweep of the letters said, *Take this man seriously.* I ran a finger across the script, to feel his power.

When I got to registration, I handed the form to the woman behind the counter, expecting quick action. I got it—she looked the form up and down, stared at me over pink half-moon glasses, and said, "Marriage and the Family is closed. You'll have to find something else." If I'd known then half of what I know now, I'd have seen it for the omen it was. But all I could think was, *I get to see Dr. Collier again.*

*O*ut on the set, Mariah spoke a line that brought my mind back to the present—it came sloshing through deep water. At that point in the script, Mariah and Biff are squaring off, and Mariah's line signals a turn for the worse. I knew what was coming. The muscles in my neck began to tighten and twist. Then the poltergeist twins really started messing with my head.

Doing the play had been risky. The script is hilarious, but a first read set me to wondering what hidden things would be dredged up if I was cast—things I maybe didn't want dredged. I had no business auditioning. Still, the day of, I went for it. I put it to myself this way: *You've spent years ducking. It's time to face down whatever comes up.*

That was before the Talbots didn't show. Before Richard went missing. My cue was coming up, and signing on to do the play suddenly seemed stupid. I dream a couple times a year that I'm in a play where I can't remember, or haven't learned, the lines. It's enough to make me nearly pee myself. As I listened to the conversation onstage, I couldn't stay focused, I couldn't keep my lines in my head. I said to myself, *If dropping lines is the worst that happens, you can count yourself lucky.*

Lucky. The poltergeist twins like that word. They tapped me on the shoulders, one on either side. *Lucky,* they echoed. *Very. You're a very lucky—*

I shook them away. Not that, not now. "Jesus Christ," I said, under my breath, "Son of God, have mercy . . ."

The show does go on. I've seen people perform sick out of their minds, or just out of them. I've seen the stage manager fill in at the last second, trundling around with the script hidden in the pages of a book. Maybe she'll remember all the blocking, maybe not. It's hard to play against someone like that—and it looks ridiculous. I mean, who reads in private anymore, let alone walks around bumping into things, their nose in a book?

Some nights on stage can be a nightmare. I didn't want to be responsible for tonight being one of them. I crossed myself. My mood didn't have to bring disaster. I'm playing Mariah's younger sister, Ariana, who's a bit thin between the ears. If my performance was scattered it would seem natural. And anyway, small-town audiences will forgive just about anything as long as there's no swearing in it.

Ariana, I thought to myself. *Ariana. Start thinking like Ariana.*

I wiped a bead of sweat from my eyelid and caught sight of my hand. It didn't even look like mine. The nails were polished. I held my hands up side by side. They looked like Gen's, my best friend in high school. Except hers were smaller. Gen kept her nails perfectly shaped and done up in mother-of-pearl. Spring of sophomore year, she cracked a pinkie nail closing her locker, cracked it so deep it never had time to grow out.

The thought gave the poltergeists a new angle. They flipped the switch on an invisible motion picture machine. Suddenly, a jerky clip, like an old eight-millimeter, played on the backstage wall.

It's that night, a Friday. Gen and I are coloring eggs. The wax crayon seems to be part of her hand, she uses it so naturally. My designs are crude. Gen's are elegant. She cradles each egg on a thin wire circle and lowers it into its bath.

There's no sound, but when her lips begin to move, I remember what she says. "Look, Claire. Look right now, while it's being born."

I look. Gen's face is shining. She could be three years old. The whiskery rabbit she's pulled out of her head looks up at us, as the shell turns blue around it.

"Claire." When I heard Paul say my name on the phone, a few weeks into spring semester, it startled me. I almost dropped the receiver. "Claire." He said it again, like he was practicing. "This is Paul Collier."

I was stunned. My mind turned into one of those revolving, crank-handle picture machines you'll see at museums. Only with the pictures out of order. You turn the crank, and the still photos come alive. I couldn't believe it. I had a new advisor in the psych department. I'd thought my Paul Collier days were done.

For our first date, we drove through falling snow to a dilap-
idated movie house in a town an hour away. It was twilight, and
the dashboard of Paul's car cast a coral-green light through the
interior. Our first kiss—which occurred at the city limits, Paul
pulling over and pulling me to him—seemed to take place un-
derwater. When I opened my eyes, the snowflakes looked like
tiny angelfish darting around.

Gen had angelfish. Her dad got them for her when he set up
his new house after he and her mom divorced. The aquarium
was behind the sofa in the TV room, where we squandered away
hours watching old movies, the fish hovering behind us.

First thing every morning, Gen and I would meet at our
lockers. One day she grabbed my arm the moment I walked up.
She put her mouth to my ear. "My dad dumped Marlena Hardwicke's mother." Marlena Hardwicke was a ghost of a girl in our
homeroom, with knock-knees. "I'm glad," she said. "That Myrtle, she's—well, you know." Gen lifted her shoulders, a shudder,
let them drop. As the bell rang and we headed to homeroom to
face the ghost girl, she summed the situation up. "Dad's seeing
a new woman now, and this one's all right. I even like it when
he brings her home."

I peeked out at the house. It was full, and there was someone I
knew in it after all: Toni Sprague-Heller. She must have come
in late. She had this fierce expression on her face and was looking like she was going to write a review. She was mentally going
down some list, weighing, considering. Not decided as to tone,
maybe. Trying on different points of view.

Great, I thought. *Just what I need. The woman who's always
intimidated me, sitting in the third row.*

I met Toni Sprague at the first dinner party Paul took me
to. She and her husband Sam were just living together then. I'd

never been to a dinner party and didn't know what to expect. Every couple there had at least one half who taught at the college. The faculty types were amazing conversationalists. But all they talked about was academics. Well, themselves and academics. Over every course: the shrimp, the soup, the rib roast, the salad—served last. The only thing in greater supply than talk was wine.

Not that I had any of it.

Hal and Kate, our hosts, didn't know what to do with me. Before dinner, Hal served every drink imaginable to everyone else, while Kate engaged me in conversation. It wasn't idle patter or insincere. She was gracious. But she clearly didn't know what to say, and it was also clear she didn't want the underage thing who was sleeping with her husband's colleague to be drinking on her premises.

"Claire," she said, "what can I get you to drink?"

I felt bad for her. I said, "A Pepsi, if you have one."

"A Pepsi," she all but sang. "Hal," she called gaily. "Would you get Claire a Pepsi?"

"Pepsi coming up."

A buzzer rang on the stove, and Kate said, "He'll be a moment, dear. He'll have to go down to the family room for that." She smiled and disappeared into the kitchen. Paul, to my surprise, had deserted me as soon as we arrived. I got left sitting alone, out of place, on a large, brown sectional sofa. I resorted to staring at my hands.

Someone sat down hard next to me. It was Sam Heller.

"So, Claire," he said. "It is Claire?" I nodded and felt encouraged enough to smile, and he said, "I've been noticing the way you smile. Your face lights up, but when your mouth first moves, it looks for just a moment like you're going to cry."

"Oh," I said. "Thanks, I guess?" The man had a smile of his own, and he knew it. I dropped my eyes back to my hands.

"Claire," he said. "Stay with me. . . . Can they go on and on, or what?" He tipped his head in the direction of the others, as if I might not know who he was talking about.

I laughed. "Well . . . they are smart."

"Yes. But you're no dumb bunny, and neither am I. Let me tell you something about this bunch. They're smart, yeah. Toni—she's scary sometimes. She can focus like no one in this world. But they got big egos. Am I right? And big insecurities. You're smiling now. . . . We're not giving them a pass because they're brains. They're just like—"

"Excuse me, Sam." Hal had appeared with my Pepsi in a chunky blown-glass tumbler. "I've got Claire's drink here." He handed it to me and shimmied away backwards. "Let me know when you want a refill."

"Thanks." I lifted the glass to my lips, but halfway, Sam extended his hand and stopped me.

"Claire. Honest now. If we weren't here, would you maybe drink something a little more interesting?"

"Well . . . maybe. I mean, sometimes."

"Now, how did I know? Let me take this for a stroll and bring it back more palatable. Pal-at-a-ble," he said, drawing out the word. "Bet you can guess I'm a whiz at Scrabble. Now, Claire, try not to call attention to yourself." He shifted his eyes toward Toni, who was deep into it with Paul, shifted them back. "Don't get me busted here."

Sam Heller saved me. He kept tabs on me, kept drawing me in. By the end of the evening, he was on my list of men I could marry. But Toni . . . By the time we finished the cheesecake, and some of us the amaretto, I was glad I hadn't been able to get into Marriage and the Family, which turned out to be her course. The woman would complicate marriage to within an inch of its life. Even with the rum Sam pilfered for me, she made me feel inferior. I made the mistake of mentioning that to Paul in the car later, and he said, "Don't blame your issues on anyone else, Claire—you're your own worst enemy." Maybe I am, but it didn't change the facts. Toni was sophisticated, she threw around words I'd hardly ever heard. And at the end of the meal, she smoked one long, skinny cigarette after another. She wasn't loud. But she liked to be the center of things. It was only her second year on the faculty, and I could see she was the darling. Of course Paul thought she was great, maybe a little too great. There was some complicated flirting going on. Toni kept making these comments that I didn't even know were funny. But they must have been. She had the table in hysterics.

When Paul had first told me about the dinner, it sounded like a lark. He said, "What do you say? We could have some fun, could put on a show. We're a couple now, and they're dying of curiosity about us."

Some show. Paul spent the night trading narratives with everyone but me.

My mother tells a story. It starts, "I had this feeling." She was in bed—alone, Dad was working graveyard shift—and all at once, she woke up. She knew someone was there. She said, "I was on my stomach, and suddenly I felt someone. I turned my head. There was a man standing beside the bed, a man with long dark hair and a long white robe. His hands were folded, crossed low in front of him. He looked at me so compassionately. . . . It was Jesus," she said.

We hadn't been to worship in a while, I don't know why. The day before had been a Sunday, and that morning Dad followed his "Rise and shine" with "Put something presentable on, we're going to church." Mom had taken communion. She ate the bread, drank the wine. She said there hadn't been anything special about it. But now, here was Jesus. When she told her mother about it the next day, Grandma said, "What do you think He was trying to tell you?" Mom didn't tell me what answer she'd given.

So . . . there was Jesus, standing by my mother's bed—Jesus, putting a whale of a dent in the universe. He put a dent in my psyche, too. I don't mind saying, I'll wake up at night and look, just to see if He's there. Wishing, I guess.

My mother was scared. She put her head down, her heart doing jumping jacks, and she kept saying in her head, *Go away. Go away, Jesus, what are you doing here?*

But Jesus wasn't fazed. Every time she dared a peek, she'd see the robe, those folded hands.

Finally, she looked again, and He was gone.

When it was my turn, Jesus didn't show. He had bigger fish, maybe. A stray thought, haphazard metaphor, a sound or a smell—real, or not—can unleash in me a hurricane of havoc, and havoc unscripted is not a good thing onstage. I tucked my hands into my armpits to warm them, barricaded the door in my brain, and listened hard for my cue. But a sudden, sharp odor of vinegar popped every nail . . .

Gen and I are at her house, coloring eggs. Her dad, Tim, and the new girlfriend are in the TV room. Outside, a car door slams. Gen looks up from the egg she's decorating, flashes a smile, and makes goo-goo eyes.

"Brett's home," she says.

She knows I think her brother is cute. She puts the egg and crayon down and flutters to the window. It's dark out, but the yard light is on. "Oh, no," she says. "What's she doing here?" I hear the front door open and close. Gen looks over her shoulder and says, "It's Myrtle. Get ready for a loony scene, with Alison here. Come on. Let's go listen."

I don't really want to, something in me doesn't like to. I shake my head and glue my butt to the chair. But Gen says,

"Come on," and pulls me by the sleeve, and I go with her. There are raised voices coming from the TV room. Tim's and Myrtle Hardwicke's. Myrtle's voice is tight, spiking high, so high, a lot of her words get lost. But we can hear enough. She calls Tim a bastard, a fucking son of a bitch, and Alison a cunt. Gen grabs my arm and gives it a squeeze. We sneak through the dark of the dining room and living room to the TV room door. I stay back from the light. But Gen moves up close.

"Myrtle," Tim is saying, "you don't need that. Put it down." He's scared—I can hear it. "You don't want to do something that will hurt anyone. Think, Myrt—think of Marlena."

Myrt says nothing.

Tim says again, "Put it down . . . Myrt." As I struggle to make sense of what he's saying, a fist closes around my heart. Alison is whimpering. The back of my neck tightens as if a hand grabbed hold from behind. Gen has inched one eye past the doorframe. She jumps back so fast she knocks us down. She rolls into me, hysterical, her voice small and right inside my ear. What she says makes my brain shut down. "A gun, she's got a gun, oh, Claire, what should we do?"

I don't have time to open my mouth. The first shot all but blows my eardrums out. Behind it is a shattering of glass, and a fishy tidal wave rolls through the doorway. My hands are to my ears. The floor could have opened—it's pandemonium. Someone is screaming. It's Alison, calling a strangled version of "Tim." Gen and I bolt for the sharp, bright lines of the kitchen door. I'm drenched and scared and can't breathe. My jaw is clamped to keep from crying out. My teeth hurt. When we get to the kitchen, it smells of vinegar and gunpowder. On the table, the Easter eggs blink blue and green, like eyes out of their sockets.

Gen pulls the wall phone off its hook. There's a second shot. "The bathroom," she hisses. "The bathroom. We can lock the door."

The phone cord is long and just fits beneath the door. Gen is breathing hard, crouched down, dialing. I'm in a hunched posture on the side of the tub. "Oh, God," she says. "Oh, God." She's rocking on her heels, her lips move silently. She's counting, waiting for someone to answer. Then her eyes bulge, her free hand flies to cover the mouthpiece. It makes no sense for her to do that. "It's dead, it's dead! It went dead!"

We sit there, looking at each other. The doorknob turns. Gen and I jump as if joined at the hip and throw our weight against the door. Our palms spread against it, our feet are planted. That's when I first notice the blue dye on her fingertips. A label from a bottle in Collin's chemistry set, Christmases ago, flashes before my eyes. Gentian violet. The third shot fires directly outside the bathroom door. The door explodes, wood splinters into and around us. It's such a surprise. *Why, I think, didn't we get out of the house?*

*O*n the set, the third shot sent a body crashing to the floor. The thud of it hitting the boards wrenched my attention out of my head and back to the show. The shots were real. They were part of the action.

Then—another shot . . . and another.

Something's wrong, I thought. The script says four shots, only four. But the part of my brain still in Gen's bathroom just accepted and watched Gen and Claire go down. It was slow motion. The last shot was there, but it wasn't. I was there, but I wasn't. One of the poltergeists stepped in and, with a bow and flourish, handed me a flower.

I'm on the floor against the bathtub, smelling lilies of the valley. For Gen's birthday, Alison gave her a box of bath beads, and it's behind me on the tub. Gen is on the floor beside me. She extends five straining, blue-tipped fingers and says, "Claire?" Her lips barely move, and I'm afraid to think why.

When I tell Richard that part, he cries.

"Claire." Someone did speak my name, but it was Lydia, from the stage crew. She touched my arm. "Claire," she whispered, "you all right? You were whimpering."

"Sorry, I'm sorry. Was I loud?"

She shook her head.

"Good," I said. "We're supposed to live the part, aren't we?" I blew across my fingers, which were freezing. My face was hot. I said, "Thanks for checking."

Lydia started to walk away. I stopped her. "Lydia, wait." She came back, and I pulled her head close. "Poke me, when I need to go on?"

"Sure."

I was having trouble focusing. I looked out on the set. The body that had fallen was on the floor, rolled into a rug. Out of the chasm in my brain a thought emerged. *I don't know who that is.* A spasm, rolling panic, rose into my throat. How could I go out on that set? Someone was down, someone was dead, and I didn't know who. I backed against the stage wall, slid down, and dropped my head between my knees. *What,* I thought, *am I doing here? I can't bear the sight of a gun, can't bear the thought of one—people use them, use them horribly, and no one does a thing. Jesus Christ, Son of God, have mercy.* The audience was laughing. Were they supposed to be? *Get a grip,* I thought. *Get a grip here, Claire.*

But—too late.

I get up off the bathroom floor and keep on going. I'm a helium balloon. I somersault, an astronaut on a tether. I float past the sink, take a right at the doorknob, go up to the ceiling. It's a rock. I bounce and think, *Cool.* I roll over and look down.

Poor things, I think.

There are bodies below. One—mine—is slumped against the wall of the tub. It's a chrysalis, abandoned, pale against the dusty rose porcelain. I think, *Is that how I look? I'm a mess.* The other body, Gen's, is sprawled across the floor. Its limbs are spread at odd angles. If you ignore the blood, she—or rather, it—looks like an Egyptian woman frozen on the wall of a tomb. *Oh, Gen,* I think.

She's not down there, though. She's at my elbow. I think, *Am I dead?*

I hear her voice in my head. *They're coming, see?* She laughs. *Come on—come on, come on.*

I don't actually see Gen. I just know she's there. Then she's not. She's gone up through the ceiling. It was such an easy thing for her to do, but I can't. I want to but I can't. I don't see anyone, either. Isn't someone supposed to come? A grandmother? An angel in white? Jesus? But I see no one.

What am I? I think. *Chopped liver?*

I scratch at the ceiling, but it stays material.

Gen, wait! I wail it in my head and start clawing at the plaster. The wail blooms into a scream. *Let me through!* I beg the molecules of the house to stand aside, but they hunker down, become obstinate, silent, dark.

The first year Paul and I were together, I drove home one night by myself to spend a weekend with my folks. It was two-lane roads, and I hit bad weather. Snow was the last thing I'd expected—the forecast had promised two days of nothing. Well, here was nothing, falling hard and heavy through the beams of my headlights. I had to keep the low beams on, to see at all, and my muscles were seized up from behind my ears to the base of my tailbone.

The farther I went, the deeper it got. Soon, a veil of snow blurred the line between the highway and the ditch, and there wasn't a plow in sight. I was locked in, four slots back in a line of cars that extended a ways behind me.

I was already half loopy from staring so hard—from steering so hard, to keep the tires in the ruts—when into the left headlight's cone of illumination came a white horse at full gallop. My jaw dropped. Time bumped into itself. The horse was velvet and ethereal in the heavy snow. It seemed to have wings. It flew though the moving line of traffic between me and the car ahead of me—its legs parallel to the ground, its blink-of-an-eye outline tinged taillight red.

Just as suddenly, it was gone.

I drove the next miles in a stupor, the only sound the squeak of my wiper blades. In the pit of my stomach, I felt touched, brushed by something I didn't understand. I noticed I had wrapped my gloved hands fiercely tight around the wheel and was still holding them that way. Not one of the drivers traveling with me braked or slowed down. Not one who had seen what I'd seen stopped to flag the others down, to say, "What did you make of that?" No. We all just drove. The farther we went, the more the wipers collected ice and the louder they got.

I heard a *thumping, thumping, thumping,* like something unsettling on the other side of a wall. With the final thump, my eyes opened. It was confusing. I was backstage, in the dark, but my eyes had opened to white—a white ceiling.

The poltergeists popped in. "Claire, you're on." No, it was Lydia. She was standing beside my bed, and Phil was at her shoulder. It was dark—the hospital—it must be night. I thought, *Did I know them then?*

Phil shook my arm. "Claire. Your entrance. It's coming up."

I remembered, then, where I was. I said, "Okay—okay."

When I came to, beside Gen's tub, there were people around me, an ambulance crew. One of them said, "You're a very lucky young lady."

I was lucky, all right. I'd lost a bucket of blood, become a labyrinth of splinters—in my body, my mind—and my picture was about to make the front page. Next to Gen's and Tim's, Alison's and . . . hers. Marlena's mother had driven down the road to the lumberyard and turned the gun on herself. I was the only survivor.

I often wonder what became of Marlena. I don't know if she had a father, one around, I mean. The week I left Paul, I had a dream. It was the sort so momentous you wake up struggling for breath. I was crossing a narrow, wooden bridge suspended between two precipices. Below me, rocks pointed dark fingers, a river frothed white. When I got halfway across, the slats of the walkway broke, and I fell through to my chest. My feet were swinging out of control. My arms were the only thing keeping me from falling, and they were weakening. "Help me," I called, the little scream of dreams. "Someone, please help me." But no one came. Just when my arms were giving way, a voice said right inside my ear, *You'll have to help yourself.* It was a voice you wouldn't say no to. It startled me. I stopped flailing and pulled myself up. I did it an inch at a time, but I did it. When my entire body was on the walkway, I lay there and breathed.

When I finally heard my cue, it was as if the voice spoke again. I pulled myself out of the pit, dusted the stage dust off, and it was enough. I hit the boards, and the moves and the lines came, from wherever they come. I opened my head, let the weight flow out, and was Ariana. The little plane flew itself. It was a newly hatched dragonfly, a rainbow on wings—more colorful, perhaps, for all the strain.

As openings go, it was fine. But by the end, I was limp. My arms ached and my legs throbbed. My head hummed. I waded to the dressing room through a heavy calm. When we gathered for notes, Phil told each of us as we came in that Marcus was dead—his heart. When we were all there, he said, "Lucy sent her apologies and hoped you were having a good show. Isn't that like her? Tomorrow's show will be for Marcus. No notes tonight, people—we'll post them tomorrow. I hope you'll give Lucy a call." We left in silence, not bouncing off the light fixtures like we usually do.

As if I hadn't endured enough. More than my share . . .

The news about Marcus was the end, the unraveled rope. It was the cornerstone pried from the wall. The opposites of my life paraded before me. Gen had been taken from me—I'd had to turn away from Paul. The one thing I wanted was to be a mother—I'm not good at even mothering myself. People, lovely, dreadful people, expect the impossible from me—I expect it in return. We call it love, all of us, broken past love. Except maybe Richard. Of the people I know, he's not quite so far past it.

He was with Lucy, of course. I thought of her, how tough and overdone she is, how fragile underneath. It had to be a blow for her. I love God, I do. Inside the shell that is me, something has always waited for God. But the thought of Lucy even close to clawing at the ceiling as Marcus went through made me sad. It made me desolate. I knew, for the first time, I was sad enough. I could stop waiting, could turn away and not look back.

By the time I got to the car, I had. I'd walked through bone-chilling wind, but I was burning up. "No more," I said. I lay my hot forehead on the cold steering wheel and cried. I didn't need a God who'd stand silently by the bed, deny you children, abandon your marriage, dangle the impossible, fail your friends . . . who would beguile you, bait you, thwart you. What was saddest was, I'd finally reached the ultimate in wild—wild with grief.

It felt good, to cry, to feel again in that way. I stopped at the all-night grocery and drifted down the aisles. When I got to the cards, I read every one in the rack. The one I chose made no mention of eternity. On its front were poppies and linden leaves, with IN SYMPATHY in tall letters. I couldn't face my empty bed, so I drove to campus. I was hurrying down the lighted path along the pond to the coffee shop when I heard wings flutter overhead and behind me. I jumped, turned, and saw, a ways off, a duck drop to the water. That calmed the unearthly tingle that had gone down my spine. The campus flock seems to stay later every year.

The coffee shop was packed. Couples on dates and scholars on break. People like me, with nowhere to go. I had to wait for a table. When I got one, I ordered hot tea with milk. I started to say, "And with honey," then I noticed the bottle on the table. As I waited, I thought hard. *How,* I wondered, *can a person ever say exactly what she's feeling?* I sat there, running different openings through my head, then dug a little notebook out of my purse. I tried, *Lucy—dear friend. You and Marcus have been so—*

Suddenly, I felt something. I felt someone, that light, that mix of heat and energy. I looked up. A woman was standing beside the table, a girl, really. She smiled and said, "Hi, I'm Molly. I'm with Campus Crusade?"

I noticed, the way her voice went up. Half of my brain thought, *Oh great—a Bible thumper.* The other half started to laugh.

Molly must have heard it. She said, "You're going to think this is crazy, maybe, but I come here a lot to talk to people, and every time I do, I pray first and ask God to tell me who. Tonight, I had a feeling He was sending me to you."

I sat there, reeling. It was the ceiling, burst open—the patient, folded hands. The laugh I was hearing in my head burbled and built. When I'd recovered my senses enough to fashion a thought, I sent out silently, *All right, I get it, I see You.* I looked into Molly's earnest eyes and said, "I don't think it's crazy at all. I've been expecting you."

She gave me a very puzzled look.

I motioned toward a chair. "It's been a long night, Molly, very long. Why don't you have a seat? Order yourself something warm. I'll tell you about it."

All This

*T*he town was quiet now.

At the VFW, the workers fried the evening's last basket of fish, then turned down the lights except those in the bar. At the cinema, the 7:45 and 8:00 screenings let out. The moviegoers streamed from every door. It was colder—they rushed to their cars. At Larkspur Theatre, the vehicles lined up again, only now at the exit to the street. Brake lights blinked on and off as drivers moved ahead. They punctuated the night.

The face of the storm was less than an hour away. Those who had come a distance for the play knew they should get right home. The train, nearing from the west, was right on time. It passed a farm, and the dog circling in the yard barked its arrival. At a neighboring house a dog answered, and then farther across the landscape, another. From the northwest, the pack announced the storm. Word of train and of storm converged on the town, it reached the lake and went beyond. But the lake already knew of the change of weather. The bay had rolled white-tipped all day. Now the waves had deepened. The sound of their rush to shore built and built.

The man stepping from his car at the church on the bluff knew what the lake was doing, though he could not see it in the dark, or hear it at this distance. He climbed the parsonage steps, opened the door. His wife, wearing a robe belted at the waist, was pouring hot water into a cup. She turned, and he pulled out a chair at the table and sat. He leaned back in the chair and began to speak. She pulled out the opposite chair and sat. There was a book on the table, open in the middle, spine up. The man leaned forward, dropped his elbows to the table, and raked his fingers through his hair. He spoke again. She shook her head. She could be saying "no"—she could be saying "oh, dear."

All this, and more, the white bird saw, flying a wider, wider circle.

Antonia Sprague-Heller

*M*y God. What a day.

There's really been only one other like it in my life. A person will struggle—she'll fight. She'll do just about anything to avoid making a decision she knows she has to make. We have got to be the most perverse creatures on the planet. Something in the human enjoys misery. It keeps us locked away, some in a mansion, some in a hovel. But then, one day—a day you don't plan, an hour you don't expect—the door opens. You have what you need, or you receive your answer. It's so obvious, and so right, and you even have the wherewithal to carry out what you need to carry out. A big angel with flaming eyes and burnished hair might as well have walked through the wall and commanded you.

I've been struggling to make a hard decision. Or, as I said, I've been struggling not to make it. When it comes to ducking and prevaricating, I've got a stack of blue ribbons. The problem is my husband. We've been separated about six months, since I caught him in an affair and threw him out. Well, that's not quite accurate. I caught him and I left. I've got my own career, a damned good one. I've got my own income. There was no sense arguing over who'd stay and who'd leave. Of course, he immediately had to do the manly thing and moved out, too. So there sat our house, empty as a tomb. I wasn't going to get into a contest to prove who could be more juvenile. I moved back in.

This past spring, two of my nieces graduated high school. They're women. I'm a woman. I figured they should know about us, so I gave them a book of quotations by women. I read one of the copies, of course, before I wrapped it. There was a real gem from Mae West: "Marriage is a great institution, but I'm not ready for an institution, yet." *Amen,* I thought. I hand-lettered it on black paper in gold ink and posted it in my office above my computer.

I didn't used to have my sense of humor in a sling. But then Sam and I separated, and I had so much anger and betrayal to process, I thought I'd implode. The first month was the worst. I washed boatloads of hankies and went through a jug of foaming bath oil. I ran up astronomical numbers on my phone bill calling my sister, who's juggling her own husband, triplets, and an administrative job. She also does committee work and volunteers for hospice, in between trips to the dentist and trilling at hockey games—oh, and scheduling grooming appointments for the Brittanies. She makes me feel like a slouch. But I carry on. A colleague in the English department told me I needed to read some books that mirror my life. He said, "The way you're feeling, you'll love *Jude the Obscure*—and *Sister Carrie* will knock you out." She did. The books were just what I needed. I had to walk on the bottom before I could find my way up.

Now most of those feelings have passed, and lately, Sam's been asking me to take him back. He's had such hope on his face every time I've seen him. I've come mere centimeters from saying, "Yes, come home." But a decision like this isn't easy, especially when there are complicating factors, like in our situation. I've been so tied to our past, so afraid of the future, I haven't been able to get on with living. Where Sam has been concerned, the only words I've seemed to know lately have been "maybe" and "maybe not." It hasn't been good for either of us. But I was too cluttered inside to make a decision.

Until tonight.

I was sitting at the desk in the kitchen, reviewing what had turned out to be an unpredictable day, when the wreckage cleared. I saw the answer. *Jesus, Mary, and Joseph,* I thought. I was so struck by the certainty that arose, I grabbed a highlighter and marked the day on the desk blotter. It's one of those giant appointment calendars. I drew a big yellow-bordered cloud with the sun breaking away behind it, right over the 13.

The other day that changed my life wasn't my wedding day, as some might expect. It, too, was a night, a night eleven years ago, and the angel who walked in wasn't very dramatic at all. He had burnished hair, yes, and a song on his tongue—but he'd come in search of trash.

When the door opened, I jumped.

I'd been deeply, solidly asleep—the kind it takes time to come out of, the kind where surfacing too fast causes physical pain. Air bubbles in the brain, or something. My office was hot and dark, lit only by the gooseneck lamp above the desk. My heart was pounding, my back and arms were numb. I shot up through levels of disorientation, eyes blurred, neck stiff and sore. The entire right side of my face felt as if it had been resting against a rock. In a sense, it had. I'd been asleep on the keyboard to my computer.

"Oh. Sorry, professor. Thought you'd gone."

It was Hank, the custodian on our floor. Everyone in the sociology department, faculty and staff, was on a first-name basis, but not Hank. He was a formal gent who insisted on using titles. His coming in surprised me. It wasn't his usual working time. I was humiliated I'd been caught sleeping, and through the fog in my brain, I could see that Hank was flustered and embarrassed. You'd have thought he'd caught me in fishnets and a teddy, whipping up a smoking flask of margaritas. He startled back from the door and said, "Had my grandson's birthday party. I'm in late. I'll come back. Didn't mean to scare you."

"No, no, Hank. It's all right. I'll step out of your way. You've got to get in here sometime, don't you?" I bolted up out of my cramped position and glanced at my watch. It had stopped. I used to throw the desk clock into a drawer when I worked late, so as not to get discouraged and not to be distracted. I said, "Do you have the time?"

"Not a question of time—I make it. It's my job."

"Of course you do. What I meant was, what time is it?"

"Gotcha." He pulled a shiny watch out of the front pocket of his vest. I'd noticed he always wore vests—it was a dapper touch I admired. He said, "My dad gave me this. It dropped out of my pocket in the movie theater once, but I found it when the lights come up. Near gave me a heart attack, 'til I had it back in my hand. It's . . . 11:43."

"Thanks."

Could it really be quarter to twelve? I thought about home, pictured my king-size bed with the sheepskin mattress pad and goose-down comforter. I pictured Sam, his arms and legs sprawled as if he owned the whole bed, which of course he did when I was cuddling with a keyboard.

Hank was a talker. He'd chitchat freely as he worked, and I usually welcomed his visits. They got me out of myself. "Little Hank, that's my grandson," he said, "turned eight today." He reached behind the desk for the recycling and the trash.

"How wonderful, Hank. Your namesake. I imagine you're close?"

"Oh, yes. He and I are train buffs. Have I told you about my trains? No? The basement's wall-to-wall tracks, with buildings and trees, people in the yards, postmen walking sidewalks, cars lined up at the crossings. There's a farm with a dog herding sheep, Canadian honkers by the pond. It's a small entire world.

The Missus spends an afternoon a week down there, dusting. She never cared a whit for a train, least not the model-sized version, 'til she met me. Now she's got her own conductor cap. You don't have much recycling today. Least, not like usual."

"No, not much."

It hadn't been going well. My recycling was usually full, the office littered with the perforated edges of computer paper. But not tonight. As Hank moved, whistling, toward his cart to empty the cans, I caught sight of my computer screen. My head hitting the keyboard had sent what I'd been working on somewhere into outer space. I'd been lucky to get in at an East Coast school and was gunning for tenure. I was also terrified I wouldn't get it—I needed all the publications I could muster. A mix of despair and fatigue bubbled up through some thinly plastered cracks. I grabbed the aspirin bottle from the top desk drawer, spun out of the room and into the hall. "Excuse me, Hank," I said as I slipped past.

"Certainly." He emptied the cans two at once and turned back into my office.

At the fountain, I palmed two aspirin, then two more, and washed them down. In the smoky, ceiling-to-floor windows lining the corridor, I caught a look at myself. I didn't like what I saw. I was only thirty—but I looked tired and stooped and harried as hell. "What are you doing?" I said to the stranger in the window. "What in piss-ant-loving purgatory are you doing, waking up in the middle of the night cuffed to a computer?"

I stared out the window at the line of light poles stretching pink-orange into the distance, and tears started to flow. Hank was now coming out of my neighbor's office, and I called out, "See you tomorrow. Gotta powder my nose."

"Sure thing, professor. Tomorrow, for sure."

I ducked into the lavatory and did my weeping in private. I didn't come out until I could tell by Hank's whistling that he'd moved into the next hall. When I got home and shook Sam awake, he took one look at my face and said, "Who died?" It took him the rest of the night to calm me down.

I enjoyed freshman year of college so much, I did it twice. Well, that's maybe not how it went. In first grade I got put ahead a year. My family is large and on the quiet side, in that way a circus can be quiet. We're half-German, from which I get my diligence, and half-Irish, from which I got my fire. I'm the baby—if you ask the others, the pampered one. Well, excuse me for enjoying being everyone's doll and turning it to my advantage. A kid would have to be pretty unskilled, in a family of eight, not to find someone to get her what she wants.

What I wanted was to read.

With seven readers in the house, I had no trouble finding a teacher whenever I wanted. I started kindergarten reading like a second grader. My teacher, Miss DuBois, didn't even try to hide her delight. She'd let me read the books for story hour.

"Antonia will read to us now," she said one day. It was just before Thanksgiving. The classroom walls were lined with strutting brown-paper turkeys with tail feathers in primary colors. I tucked my feet beneath me to rise from my rug but froze when a complaint clobbered me from behind.

"She read to us yesterday." It was Johnny J., my kindergarten nemesis, not to be confused with Johnny B., a boy who never caused me any grief. Johnny J. had risen from his rug, unbidden. His flaxen hair was standing straight up, weaving in a river of static.

"Didn't you like the book Antonia read, Johnny?" Miss DuBois said.

"Yeah. But I want to read today."

"You're not quite ready."

"I am, I can read," chirped Natalie Bean. Her hand shot up, waving. "Cat. C-A-T. Dog. D-O . . . uh . . ."

"G. Very good, Natalie. When you've learned more words, it'll be your turn. Antonia, come." Miss DuBois motioned me forward. "You may choose a book."

"Again?" came from Johnny. He gave a loud groan of sorrow and pain.

"Johnny," Miss DuBois warned. Johnny J. had jumped to his feet and was en route to the bookcase. "Back to your rug, please. John Jessup—your rug."

"Ohhh," Johnny expelled through set teeth. He flopped his butt down hard onto his green rug and speared me with a scowl.

Not quite a year later—fat jack-o'-lanterns were dancing across the classroom walls—the principal summoned my parents to a conference. At its conclusion, I'd been advanced a grade starting in January. I'm not sorry to report, when Master Johnny J. heard about it, he all but writhed on the floor.

As I contemplated starting college, I wanted the hell out of Dodge. I come from a comma of a town near Minot and Grand Forks—that would be North Dakota—and I was ready for Exclamation Point. I chose Wisconsin, at Madison. I have family not far from there, my father having grown up in Door County. The UW offered everything I could want—distance, drama, and weekends with my grandparents.

I've spent life pretty much inept around men. It started early, by not starting. I was fifteen before I had my first visit from my friend, what girls back then used to call their periods. I'd been watching, wishing for that first one, but when it arrived, I was at a loss. It came on so commonly, so coarsely. I had longed so, but the sensation I felt as I crossed over was that of falling out of a swing. My body was barely changed outwardly, its inner workings hidden. As the fact of the red smear in the crotch of my panties made its way to my brain, I felt, surprisingly, grief. Something wondrous had come, but I recognized instantly and with regret that something wondrous had gone.

I didn't know what to do. So I got rid of the evidence. My mother has this unfailing radar. Within hours she had found the stain in the tangle of the hamper and come to me, panties in hand. She'd been out painting windows and was wearing one of my father's work shirts. She looked beautiful. The shirt was untucked, her hair up in a kerchief. One strawberry strand had come loose and had paint on it. She'd apparently brushed it back with her hand.

"Toni," she said. "Why didn't you tell me? It's nothing to be ashamed of. You need to rinse these in cold water or the stain sets."

I wasn't sure how I felt about it and looked away. My chest was swelling with some kind of emotion, and tears were gathering.

Mom circled her arms around me. "You're okay, sweetie. It takes getting used to, I know. But it's just part of growing up." Of course, she's never been one to let pass a chance to tease. She said, "If you kiss a boy now, you'll have a baby."

I was mortified, thrilled.

That evening over pot roast and glazed carrot spears, she announced meaningfully to my father, "Our little girl has become a woman." I don't know who was more red-faced. Him, or me.

By my freshman year in college, men were completely mysterious to me. I've always been excitable, and I didn't know which would be worse—approaching a guy or being approached. Either way, I knew I'd squirm and expire on the spot. But I was on a mission to find my soul mate, and I brushed my hair a hundred strokes each night and doused myself each morning with baby powder perfume. Sort of a pre-embalming ritual.

The first week of October, I packed my books and headed for Helen White Library. It was Saturday, the day a glory. Sunshine was gilding the campus, leaves blowing on the trees. I walked through a breeze that smelled of late grasses and flowers.

It was tempting, from my study carrel next to a window on an upper floor, to go out into the world below, but I stayed where I was, scratching through draft four of a descriptive essay. A trip to Helen White wasn't only about studying. I was trawling for studious men, and at the next carrel sat a modern Adonis.

I wore glasses then and had taken and slipped them into my backpack, but I still managed to slide into the carrel gracefully. The point is, the old eyeballs weren't seeing much. But the heart was. Adonis had olive skin and hair curled black over his collar, and his eyes—no lie—they smoldered.

I needed to get noticed.

I leaned back in my chair, staring into the void above my prose like a classic film legend. I twirled and untwirled my hair. Suddenly the divider between the carrels melted away, and I leaned toward my object. He turned, surprised. My hair was long, and it fell forward of my shoulders, spilled spellbindingly red onto his arm. It bewitched him. His arm lifted—slow, inevitable—and wound its way into my tresses. His eyes bored into mine, as with a slow, tingling, rapturous pull, he moved my lips toward his. My heart went berserk.

My real heart.

In real life. The rest I'd imagined.

A vein started to thrum in my temple. *Thrum, thrum. Thrum, thrum.* I was having trouble breathing. I knew if I stayed, I might flop like a rag doll to the desktop. I foresaw a crowd gathering, scrutinizing me like a species of insect, and I slammed my glasses onto my face and crammed my essay into my pack. Adonis looked up, finally—looked away—checked his watch. I got up and bolted. The speed of my exit made the bag checker at the door finger through my pack with extra care.

Call me the Queen of Irony.

On Halloween morning, I ended up at health services. Antonia Sprague, whose virgin lips had never been touched, who'd gotten no closer to a guy than a carrel away, had mononucleosis. Spit-swapper's disease. I was struck by the injustice of it—to suffer the humiliation of implied sin, without having bathed in the pleasure.

That was the end of my first freshman year. My parents jumped into the pickup and came to collect me. When I'd recovered, I ferried plates at the local truck stop. The regulars called me Stretch. "Whoa, didn't see you there, Stretch. Told you about that standing sideways. Say, Stretch. How about another cup of joe?" That job was the best thing that could have happened to me. I realized not everything worth something is in books. But books come close. By August, I had mastered the contact lens and was flush with cash. As I hung up my apron to go back to Madison, I knew I'd go to school forever, to sling ideas instead of hash.

I was also already thinking the whole fifties, sixties mom thing wasn't for me—and when I met Sam, he felt the same way. About fatherhood, I mean. Deciding not to have kids has been interesting. An acquaintance at church took my hand one morning, gave me a grandmotherly smile, and pressed a slip of paper into my palm. On it was written, in a careful but unsteady hand, MARK LOFTUS, MD, followed by a downstate phone number. Mark Loftus is a local boy who made good. He's also a fertility specialist.

I'm amazed that I fit in at church. My colleagues—a few, I mean—think me intellectually deficient for being there. There's a pelican on the roof, for God's sake. Well, yes—that pelican gives me hope. It's outside the box. I don't know that God exists, and I'll say so. Half the people in the pews would say the same if you put the screws to them. I can't look to the Bible, chapter and verse. I was maybe ten when I stopped reading it literally. There's a legend around the church that one of the pelicans that inspired its founding is still out there. People see it, here and there. It's a mysterious and lovely idea. Aside from what the pelican might mean—because, who knows—do we say it's there because it is, and we know it intuitively? Or is it there because we say it is—we create the reality? Either way works for me. It's the questions that matter, not answers. To stop wrestling with questions is a kind of death. There's something in me beyond reason, though—something like whatever brings the monarch back to its wintering grounds, to the very trees its great-great-greats left at the start of the migration.

Last summer, I was driving back from a trip to my brother's. I was in a long line of cars moving through a construction zone. The car ahead of me veered to the right, and I saw why. A kitten had been hit—it lay to the left of the lane. As I passed, it raised its head—just its head—and its mouth opened. A last, imploring O. I couldn't stop. I couldn't help. For the next hour I wept and drove and railed at God. I believe, without doubt, that the kitten and I are part of a whole. As long as some church somewhere believes in it, serves it, and allows someone like me, I'll be there.

When I think of God, or whatever name you know God by, I have to go to metaphor. If there's a divine being, it's out there, yes, watching over, but for me it's more like that wolf on a dark, snowy hillside you'll see in prints in antique shops. My Grandpa Sprague had the wolf print on the wall of his library. I used to sit and stare into its blue-green world for hours. There was something distant and comforting about it. I was drawn by the cold slope of the hill, the wolf's steaming breath, so real I could hear it. I was mesmerized by its one visible eye shining over the shadowy cabins below. The wolf loved them. It loved the snow-covered roofs, the light yellow and warm in the windows. They belonged to him.

That's God to me. If there is a God.

I met Sam at a political rally my last year of grad school. He's just shy of five-foot-ten—I quietly gave up heels when we met—

and has California-surfer hair, slightly thinning on top, hazel eyes, and a smile so charming it'll defrost a Deepfreeze at a thousand paces. I gave up cigarettes because of that smile—well, that, and his being an unrelenting nudge—though it took a few years. I started smoking in graduate school, more for the buzz than the image, though the image did confer its own buzz. The cigs had this implacable power. All I had to do was see some femme fatale or studly sweet cheeks light up in a movie, and I'd feel, like a sweat, nicotine hitting the blood. I never smoked in the house, once Sam and I moved in together. I stood outside in blizzards, pouring rain, heat warnings—I haunted the garage at thirty-below, sucking in one more drag. But Sam has powers, too. The smokes didn't stand a chance.

At the time we met, I'd had very few . . . well, I can't even call them relationships. Sam is four years older. Those few years made him not intimidated by my mind, the way guys my own age had often been. I don't say this out of conceit. Whether you've got looks or brains or charm, you generally figure it out and use it. I do what I can, fashion-wise, but I'm no model. There are no cheekbones to die for here. I realized, early on, I wasn't cut out physically or mentally for gliding around with a book on my head.

My family has always been proud of me, in that conflicted way families have. As a kid, I could get straight A's, yet be confounded by the simplest mechanical task. I lost an hour once, trying to change the thread on a bobbin. My mother grew up in a community where sewing in women was second nature. She'd misplaced the manual to her sewing machine, or thrown it away. She didn't need it. I was a different case—without directions, I was flummoxed. Mom finally changed the thread for me.

I probably seemed a little strange. I'd read anything, anywhere—bulletin boards, circulars in the mail, traffic signs, the backs of cans. I'd read standing, squatting, in odd sprawled postures across my bed at two in the morning, slumped in the big armchair with my feet on the wall above my head. I'd read in the tub, crowded on the bus, packed into the car, walking down the sidewalk, even washing dishes with a book propped open behind the sink. When it got too loud in the house, I'd go to the garage and hide in the passenger side foot well of the car.

Mom would find me there. "Toni, what are you doing here again? Go outside—get some sun."

"I'm reading."

"I see that. But you've got an odd smell, and you're shedding spores. I just vacuumed this car."

"All right." I'd exhale, dramatically, to emphasize how inconvenienced I was, get my sunglasses and a hat, and plant myself beneath a tree, where I'd read some more.

Sam's a reader, too. But he limits himself to sci-fi and factual stuff. He's a logical, grounded, male-brained person. He's a lot like my father, who's a school psychologist. I'm a sucker for the type—I also have a slant toward things logical. But I've got a definitely female way of communicating. I occasionally just need someone to listen. I need to rant and cry and blow off steam. But Sam can't stop himself from offering some sort of solution. It annoys the piss out of me. Through our entire separation, he's never given up suggesting answers to my problems. Even about the men I've been seeing. You'd think he'd know better.

So often when I need to talk, I wish my family were closer. Geographically, I mean. News from home comes mostly by phone. Dad's on the telephone a lot at work and is no fan of it at home, so I talk mostly with Mom. Our conversations are so leveling, so interesting. "Guess what?" she said one day. It was spring—Sam and I were still back East. "Your father and I have decided to get some ducks." They'd ordered four ducklings from the feed store and were building a shelter by the pond.

"The pond?" I said. The whole thing seemed questionable to me. Winter is diabolical in the Dakotas—even the fish head indoors. "What about next winter?"

Without the slightest hitch in her voice, Mom said, "I'm clearing a spot in the freezer." As if she and Dad regularly be-headed the brood around their table.

"Mom," I said. I'd helped my grandmother slaughter enough chickens to be thinking this wasn't a good thing. "Who's going to put them there?"

"We will. We think raising them will be fun, a return to our childhoods. You'd think you were talking to city folks, or something."

Some weeks later, Mom reported the ducklings had ar-rived—two females, two males. They lived at first in a box in the house. Our next conversation was dominated on Mom's side by hilarity and disgust. She described the birds' voiding into their own water and food, the way they then ate and drank with relish.

For some reason I've never understood, considering the ducks' future, Mom announced they had named them. When the weather warmed, it wasn't the ducks that went out. It was Patience and Temperance and Courage and Fortitude who moved into the little house by the pond, where—according to Mom—they carried on happily.

By July, Mom was reporting weird things about Temper-ance. She'd swim the circumference of the pond and go into a spin. Her head would pull back and to the right, as if she were in a vise. Her body would convulse, her path would devolve into smaller and smaller circles until during one episode she went under, her legs sticking up, beating the air. The other ducks sent up a call of distress and swam in a tight little pack. Hearing and seeing it all from the window, Dad did a record sprint and pulled Temperance back.

The only birds I was seeing were pigeons. Sam and I were living in an apartment in an eight-unit building that had once been a house. In its glory days, it had been the family home of some wealthy, unnamed urbanite. It had a wide central staircase that at some point had been walled down the middle by an enterprising landlord. The nearby river, crapped up and smelly despite a reclamation project, wound dutifully through what had once been the elegant part of town.

We didn't have a yard. Out back was a parking lot with a large tree paved into the middle of it. Out front were two bushes, each entertainingly surrounded by a white picket fence. A mere three steps would put someone who was leaving out into the street.

The next time Mom called, they'd lost Temperance. The duck had another spell, and no one was at hand. By the time Dad heard the other ducks wailing and beat it up from the barn, it was too late. There was no reviving her.

The loss, for me, was a distant one, but it hit me. To make it worse, I went out to the parking lot the next day and found a pigeon huddled in the corner where the concrete step joined the house wall. It was lame in one leg and missing feathers. From the look of things, the other birds had turned on it and pecked bleeding ulcers into its skin.

We didn't socialize with our neighbors. There was an unspoken agreement everyone should keep to themselves. But there was this woman, June—I'd guess in her sixties—from apartment one, who was as drawn to the pigeon as I was. I knew from her mailbox her last name was Mancini. I'd observed, in long bouts of loitering at the window, that she and her husband lived with a woman about their age who seemed somehow disabled. I'd watched them help her into and out of their car.

"A shame," June said. We were fretting over the pigeon, and June straightened up and wiped her hands on her dress.

She'd been trying, without luck, to get the bird to eat something. "I hate when a living thing ends up like this."

"My parents have ducks," I said. "One just drowned. A fit of epilepsy or something."

"A duck? Drowned? Don't that beat all. This fellow's not looking too good, either. It bothers me to think of him huddled here all night. He's cat food in the making. Can't take him in, though—not a wild bird. He could spread some kind of disease. With Iris, I can't take a chance."

"Iris?"

"My sister. She's been with us since Ma died. It's going on five years. Ma said her labor with Iris was hard, and very long. Iris . . . well, she's walked a different road. Nowadays that doesn't happen so much. You want kids?" she said.

"Uhhh, well. I don't know. I mean, it's not something we're talking about."

"Talking don't do it, dearie."

When I got home from school the next evening, the bird was gone. I'd known, somehow, it would be, but my heart dropped anyway. There were lights at June's. I knocked. As soon as she saw me, she put an arm around me. "Toni. Come in. Iris and I are having some coffee. Can I get you some? Look, Iris. It's Toni from upstairs. She was tending that bird with me."

June's kitchen was hot and smelled of beef stock and yeast. Iris looked up from the table. She was holding her cup solidly in both hands, and she put it down carefully and nodded. "Br-rrrr," she said. It startled me. "Brrrrr," she said again.

"No," June said. "I meant the bird with the hurt leg."

I wasn't following the conversation. Iris picked up the cup again and drank without taking her eyes off me. "Brrrrr," she said, and this time the syllable had a demanding pitch. June laughed.

"Oh, she doesn't want to see that old thing, Iris."

There was no satisfying her, though, and June finally said, "She wants to show you her room. She's got something in there she likes to show to people."

"Oh. All right."

June helped Iris up from her seat. She said, "She has trouble with her balance." I trailed behind, June and I taking one slow step for every three or four of cautious Iris's.

When we got to her room, Iris grabbed me by the hand and steered me to a birdcage hanging by her bed. Its door hung open, and the bottom was lined with pink floral shelf paper. Taped to the hanging perch, as if on a high trapeze, was a picture of two girls about middle-school age. It was an old picture—grainy and yellow with age. Iris gestured at it, slid a hand to the back of my neck, and guided me to a closer look.

"That's her and me," June said. She shook her head. "When Moko, my parakeet, died, I cleaned the cage and set it by the door for Ben to take to the basement. But Iris took it in her head she had to have it in here. When I saw what she'd done, I took the picture out, but she got really mad and put it back in. I just left it. She likes to sit in that chair there and look at it." June swooped up what looked like underwear, peeking out from under the bed. "Wouldn't you like to know what would make her do such a thing?"

After all these years, I still think about Iris, that uninhibited and authentic way she reached for me and pulled my head exactly where it needed to be. I think about June, who was exactly where she needed to be. I know I'll never see them again. But they're forever in my head. As for the ducks . . .

My parents couldn't bring themselves to slaughter them. They gave them to my uncle, who invited them for duck dinner and received a fast refusal.

After our breakup, Sam couldn't accept that I might not get over what had caused it. We've met for breakfast at least once a week, and one morning the waitress skittered up to the table with a tower of dirty plates balanced in her arms. She was young and in a flurry. People were stacked up like cordwood, waiting for empty seats. She dropped the plates onto our table and whipped out her order book. "What can I get you?"

"A cup of coffee—" I began.

"With cream," Sam finished.

I shot him a look. "Since when have you started ordering for me? Do your dates these days suffer some sort of disconnect between the mouth and the brain?"

"My dates?" he said. He beamed a smile at the waitress, who wore MARY in black letters over her left breast. "Mary," he said. "Would you want to stay married to someone this delightful in the morning?"

Mary blushed under the smile. She looked disconcerted. "Uhhhh," she said and glanced toward the pass-through window, clearly hoping somebody's omelet was up.

"Well. I would," Sam said.

Dream on, I thought. I flipped a page of the menu.

Sam laughed. "I'll have coffee, too, Mary. How about you get that? Then we'll order."

Mary slid the order book into her pocket and swept up the syrupy plates. When she'd gone, Sam said, "It bothers you."

"What?"

Truth was, anything he said or did bothered me. But he didn't need to know.

"That I could be seeing someone."

"Sam," I said. I knew the affair was over. He'd told me, and I'd heard it independently via the grapevine. He stopped seeing her right after I moved out. "I wouldn't care if you were seeing the Queen of England."

"Rang her up. She doesn't go for California boys."

"Well, that's good for England. It's good to have intelligence in your queen."

He abandoned the playful approach. "Toni. Don't you see I'm waving a white flag here?" He leaned across the booth—his hand nearly connected with mine. I pulled it away, reached for a napkin. "Look," he said. "I've got it coming, I know it. Anything you want to throw at me, I deserve. You want to call me a son of a bitch? Go ahead. Paint my portrait in camel dung? Baby, I'll buy it—I'll hang it on my office wall. What's it going to take? What, Toni, do I have to do?"

"I don't know what you have to do," I said. "I don't know what I'm going to do. All I know is it fucking hurts."

Two coffees clattered onto the table from half a foot up. Three containers of half and half rolled like a craps throw behind them. Sam caught one just as it skittered into his lap and flashed Mary a grin. "No cream for me, thanks."

"Sorry," Mary said. She flipped the order book open and said, a little fearfully, "You two decided?"

*H*ow could a woman not fall for Sam?

His field is actuarial science. At the time we met, he was working for a big insurance company in town. After the rally, a bunch of us went out for coffee, and I told Sam I was a grad student in sociology. He brightened. "We're a perfect match," he said. "Think about it—we're both interested in statistics and patterns. You with your hair cinched up in the ivory tower, me getting my pencil dirty in the real world."

I thought, *What a charmer.* And as I thought it, I knew I could marry him. Sam's got his own ideas. I haven't worn my hair in a bun a day of my life—I wouldn't be caught dead in one. He knows it. But he loves giving me grief, and he loves emphasizing that real world thing, as if he really and truly believes that everyone who teaches at the college level has their pinhead up their ass and Flubber on their shoes. We went around and around about it. Sam saw at once it was a button to push.

So much for soul mates. I like haute cuisine. Sam accommodates that by buying a bird-hunting license every year and serving partridge under glass. But on his own he'll go for spaghetti or burgers. I'm inclined toward concerts or the theatre—he'd rather take in a pro game or go fishing. I'll take Mozart, Bach, or Sibelius. Sam will listen to anything. He was on a Todd Rundgren kick the year we met. For our one-month anniversary, he stood on my porch with a little yellow guitar and serenaded me with a sexy rendition of "Hello, It's Me." The song was already an oldie, but the lyrics were right. I've always been guilty of thinking too much, and it's about right that Sam and I would choose as our song one about a failing relationship.

Not long after we were married, we had a bizarre episode. In bed one night, a spinning, silver disc burrowed into Sam's cranium. We'd been asleep, and he started screaming. I had never heard anything like what was coming from the man next to me. I was sure, if Sam's voice pitched any higher, his vocal cords would snap.

"Sam," I said. I placed one hand firmly on his shoulder, so as not to startle him. "Wake up. You're dreaming." My touch, my voice, had no effect. I shook him, said, "Sam. *Wake up.*"

His screaming stopped in one shocked inhalation. He snapped to a sitting position and brought his hands to his head. He said, in a voice that sounded stoned, "Something like the blade of a circular saw came spinning at me out of the dark—it tore into my forehead just above my nose. I did not want that thing in my head. If it . . . Jesus . . . if it got in, I'd be dead."

"It was a dream," I said, to reassure him. I've since come to understand it—the abject fear of extinguishment that jerks one from sleep. But that night I didn't. I lay awake until the window shade hovered rectangular and white, the tape in my head stuck on *What is he afraid of?*

I love to tell people about Sam's trip to Boston to visit his brother. He left on Sunday and came back on Friday—it wasn't like he was strapped for time. As a memento, he brought me a potholder that looked like Paul Revere's lantern. I thought, *Where'd he get this? Not Beacon Hill.* I laughed and hung it over the stove. I made a big thing out of using it every day, and an even bigger thing out of showing it to some ladies from church when I had them over. Most of them smiled politely. A few actually liked it. Mabel Gunderson oohed and aahed. She said, "Paul Revere! Oh, for cute." My friend Rena, who was my roommate when I went back to Madison, busted up, laughing. Her husband, Richard—who she was dating back then and who I used to juggle potatoes with, they were flying between us—is now pastor at Pelican. That's the name of our church, hence, the bird on the roof. Rena complained endlessly about finding spuds under all the furniture. It was Richard's apartment—I don't know why she was cleaning over there. She looked at Sam's lantern potholder and said, "He brought you that? With the entire metropolis of Boston to choose from, he brings you that?"

I cocked my head and raised an eyebrow. It said, *Whatever do you mean?* The other ladies missed it, but Rena read it like I'd penned it on the counter top. We know each other well . . . almost too well. We've seen each other on some not-so-good days. She poked at the potholder with a look of disgust. "I'd put a good deal of thought into the next gift I gave Sam Heller, if I were you. Get my drift?"

I did.

I put a lot of thought into it. I can be very good at putting thought into things. The potholder theme appealed to me. It was familiar, yet inspired—the possibilities were endless. Every household should have potholders hanging on squadrons of nails. Sentimentalized, commercialized, in any sort of bad taste.

What more unique expression of a unique relationship? The next time I left town, for a conference in Omaha, I scoured the city for the tackiest I could find.

In the wrapped and beribboned box I presented to Sam was a smiling, stuffed-steer oven mitt with a stalk of wheat in its teeth, the package guaranteeing the mitt to be entirely fireproof. I won't tell you what Sam's first sight of it prompted him to say. Nor did I stop there. Sam has in his possession today the most well thought out, most horrific potholder collection in existence. It's been a source of satisfaction to me, and an ongoing lesson for him. Do unto your wives, oh ye husbands, as you would have them do unto you.

It's been said, "Don't get mad, get even." Well, I'm here to report, if you do it creatively and with a light heart, revenge is as good as sex. Of course, the reverse is also true. Sex—it's the best revenge.

I've had two relationships since Sam and I separated. The shorter and more recent one was with a man named Warren, twelve years my senior. Warren is charming and thoughtful— but he was in bed, without fail, every night at ten. And I do mean in bed, asleep. Still, we had some fun. He took me to his father's sixtieth high school reunion. I loved listening to the class members' stories. They'd seen amazing changes in sixty years. The end to the evening was especially memorable. A one-man band, accordion and harmonica, performed every hit from the thirties. I mean every one. It was a far cry from Paris—there's nothing like it in the Big Apple.

The relationship before Warren was with a man twelve years my junior. The two were like book ends. Now, I didn't set out to get laid by a younger man. The opportunity simply presented itself. After the separation, I signed up for yoga. It was innocently done. I was out of shape and feeling stressed. My instructor—

I'll call him Pete—turned out to be gorgeous. He could do things on a sticky mat I hadn't dreamed possible. His adho mukha svanasana would turn a woman's legs to K-Y Jelly. In English, that would be his downward-facing dog.

Pete was an alluring combination of types. He had the trim, muscular body of a Marine and the long hair and laid-back manner of the sprouts and granola club. Our class met in the evening. It was late June, and one night was so hot and humid the air-conditioner in the studio could barely keep up. After class, I did a quick change out of my yoga clothes while Pete was changing his. The timing was perfect. I bumped into him coming out of the johns and walked out with him. Flashing what I hoped was a beguiling smile, I said, "Pete. Would you like to have a drink? I'm buying. That is, if drinking's not against your philosophy."

He must have known I was hot for him. He smiled this Buddha-like smile and narrowed his eyes. "Do you never," he said, "violate your own philosophies?"

The way he used the negative in the question—coupled with how close he was to me—threw me. I stammered, "I . . . I suppose."

"Let's go."

I took him to La Crème, a quiet club known for its upscale clientele. It was wonderful. I hadn't felt that way for a long time— I was intoxicated—and it wasn't the two Golden Cadillacs that had rolled into my garage.

Oh, why be coy? I took him home with me. Sam would have shit if he'd known, which made it that much better. The AC was out and the house was a furnace, but we hardly noticed. We didn't even make it to the bedroom. Pete pulled his yoga mat and roll out of his bag—the roll is this stuffed fabric tube— unrolled the mat on the living room rug, and flopped next to it, cross-legged. He patted the floor suggestively. "Let's do a little yoga." I dropped beside him like Plato at the knees of Socrates.

Despite the heat, I was wearing my new beret—it makes me feel hot, the other kind of hot. Pete snatched it from my head and tossed it over his shoulder. "Something simple," he said and centered the roll on the mat. "How about blades above the roll?"

I wish there were Sanskrit for that, but there's not. It's not a classic yoga pose. I squiggled onto my back and positioned the roll below my shoulder blades. I knew why he'd chosen the pose. It lifts the breasts. It felt luxurious and wicked to arch back and let him admire me. Ever the good student, I completed the pose by stretching my legs languidly and reaching overhead, letting my arms fall into a position of rest.

"Very good." Pete spoke it right into my ear. "Now. Don't move." His hands began to ripple across my body, teasing, exploring. At first, he kept them outside my clothes, but then he slipped them underneath. "Toni. No moving."

It was the most tremendous blades above the roll I'd ever experienced. Pete brought it to a glorious head by sliding onto me and drawing little circles with his pelvis. Everywhere. He was supple, he was firm. I thought I'd die. I pushed him off and began peeling out of my clothes. He watched, as if he had stepped back, then crossed the space between us in one fluid motion, his lips a swarm at my breasts, glazing, nibbling. Just as my lips were opening to beg, he covered them with his, then pulled free and drew his t-shirt up and over his perfected shoulders. His chest was tanned and glistening in the heat. I swear, he smelled like the woods in spring.

All he was wearing then was a pair of white shorts. I'd already surmised there was nothing underneath. By all that's tender, lovely and true, it seemed a shame to take them off. They did the man justice. His thighs were faultless, with soft blond hairs that stood out against the skin. But as summer follows spring, the shorts came off. . . . How shall I put this? There's a physical trait that can be thought of as the signature of a man, and Pete had an impressive one. It scrawled, it astonished, it turned me giddy, almost scared. It was good I wasn't my younger self, or I might have run from the room. As it was, I briefly considered it. Pete pulled a plastic package out of a zippered compartment in his bag. It was a condom, something I hadn't seen in years. He unwrapped and handed it to me. "Some parts of one's philosophy," he said, "must never be violated."

Pete and I could tussle like minks, but we had nothing to say to one another. Positively, absolutely zero. It was too bad—I mean, consider the possibilities. Maybe it was the age difference again, but it didn't last. The euphoria dissipated in about four weeks.

The crash-and-burn Hank triggered when he barged into my office took place a couple years after Sam and I had moved in together. He'd relocated with me, but we were avoiding marriage religiously. I had my reasons to be wary of it—he had his. Those were the days before answering machines, and I used to turn off the ringer on my phone. I had to. People are one strange animal—they don't know when to give up. It would set my teeth on edge to be hard at work and to hear this strident ringing, ringing, in the background.

As a partner, I was pathetic—I can admit it. I loved being with Sam, but by my schedule. The rest of the time was Toni Time. Sounds like a beer commercial. At least once a day, I'd pull myself away from my office and inhale some sort of gut bomb on campus. If Sam hadn't stopped at the market, at home we'd have starved. No mice took up residence at the Sprague/Heller place. No bright-eyed little faces peeked out of our cupboards. Any mouse domestic unit foolish enough to have moved in would have vacated before the month was out, reduced to rodent skin and bones. And they'd have been grateful to be getting out at all, the human members of the household having a voracious look.

Like all men, frankly, Sam can be a prick.

But I've got to give him credit. He doesn't mind a turn in the passenger seat, and, except for the obvious lapse of the affair, he's generally more attuned to my state of mind than I am. On the evening Hank walked in on me, Sam had showed up at my office around dinnertime. He'd gone to Chang's for takeout, and the sack he was carrying sent out a strong odor of ginger chicken, my favorite.

"C'mon, Toni," he said. "Let's take it home tonight. Blame it on me, tell anyone who gives you shit that it's my fault. Say I'm lonely, I guilted you. Say I convinced you, against your better judgment. Better yet—tell 'em to stick their damn publications."

I felt my arms being yanked in opposite directions.

"I can't. You know I can't. They could get rid of me tomorrow and have a hundred takers the following day. I've got to keep at it. I've got to make them want to keep me."

My loyalties were a little misplaced, but Sam didn't say it. He shrugged and snapped open the takeout. "Whatever you say." We ate without talking. A couple of times, he took away the printout I was working on when I picked it up.

Later, as I stood at the hall window listening to Hank's whistling, the squeaky wheels of his cart, I saw my error in a sickening rush. Outside, steam was curling out of the grates that lined the perimeter of the building, and as I watched the patterns it made, I didn't even want to keep myself. I couldn't get home to Sam fast enough. Before he changed his mind.

The next day I called in sick—called in well, is how Sam put it—and when I went back, things were different. I began to enjoy life. I started a job search, and we eventually moved here. It's been a good move—small town, small college. It's not the most diverse place, but even here people can surprise you. Sam and I surprised ourselves and got married, a couple years after the move. We set about cultivating a yellow-bungalow, picket-fence kind of relationship and came precariously close to traditional norms. We even almost got a dog, until I came to my senses.

The way I found out about his affair was a joke. We'd drifted into complacency. I'd known all about midlife crises, especially the notorious ones in men, but Sam had passed forty without a splash. By the time he hit forty-five, or it hit him, I wasn't paying any attention at all.

He must have wanted to get caught. In April, he left a note from the egg-sucking weasel in the back pocket of his pants. Sam usually did the laundry. I pitched in, oh, I'll be generous and say twice a month. It was on one of those occasions I found it. In my family, growing up, it was unforgivable to read something addressed to someone else. We just didn't. But this situation was different—there was a judgment call to make. Was it something important, or something to toss? I unfolded the note, glanced it over, and then read it again and again. There was no way around it. It was what it was. The tone was so intimate, the text so riddled with inside jokes, I knew he was sleeping with her. I crumpled it, burst into tears, then smoothed it back out. I stared at it. What should I do? I'd been hit by a Mack truck, and my rational processes had ridden out of town splattered across its grille.

I'd like to say that when Sam got home we sat down and discussed it, calmly, but who'd believe that? I met him at the door with my overnight bag packed. I shook Exhibit A in his face. "I suppose you have an explanation?"

He saw what it was, and his whole body got quiet. "I love you," he said, "only you." He didn't even attempt an explanation. The rat. "It just happened," he said. I found out later it was someone from work. I walked out without another word.

I headed for Rena's. Since she and Richard got together, we haven't been the friends we were. She . . . she cut me out. Richard was the first guy she dated that I didn't think a total butthole. I had a little crush on him myself, but . . . don't take this wrong . . . I was in love with Rena, not physical, not sexual, but a deep attachment, and I think, until Richard, it was the same for her. I still love her. When Pastor Jack left, there was this tidal wave of grief. I knew Richard had the sort of heart that could step into a situation like that and turn it around, so I gave them a call. I guess I hoped things would be different between us. They weren't. Still, Rena was the only one I was going to when I found out about Sam. Richard wasn't home. He was doing hospital visits, and I was glad. I didn't even make it through the door without crumbling. One look at Rena standing in it, and I burst into tears.

"What is it?" she said.

"Sam. What else?"

I don't know what I was hoping for from her, but it wasn't what I got. She sat me down. "Want some tea?"

"Yes, something soothing. I've had a day from the back forty of Hell." I took a deep breath and spilled the godawful mess. The laundry, the pocket surprise, Sam's strange, disconnected admission. When I was done, Rena just sat there, silent. She shifted in her chair, she seemed uncomfortable. I didn't know what to make of it. Was she reacting to me, or the situation? I suppose it's hard to hear of trouble in a friend's marriage without feeling a little uncertain in your own. Even being married to a minister is no guarantee the course of true love will run smoothly. Rena's reaction struck me as strange. When you really know her, you know quiet is not Rena's strong point.

Our first day as roommates, she walked in and I was immediately put off. Not by her exactly, but her presentation. She bounced in, laughing and chattering, with holes in her jeans and a string of love beads around her neck. Everything about her said flower child, except she was the opposite of laid back. I could see she was used to being popular.

"I'm Rena Capshaw," she said.

Even her name was perky. To makes things worse, she had blue eyes and hair that was straight, shiny and blonde. But I soon saw that beneath it all she was as vulnerable as I was, and it made me feel close to her. We studied together, watched guys together, talked late into the night over pizza and beer. The guys Rena saw didn't interfere with us. She kept them apart. But then she met Richard. Not only did I have to share my best friend, but I had to sit there and watch her change. If I tried to talk to her about it, she got testy. "MYOB," she'd say.

The irrepressible Ms. Capshaw slit the wrists of her deepest self to fit some idea of a pastor's wife. Now, I think clergy and their families ought to get million-dollar salaries. Most of them labor away, under-appreciated, never measuring up in some quarter or other. But I'm talking about my friend. To this day, I don't understand what Rena was thinking. She made herself into a woman the girl in love beads wouldn't have liked. It felt like she left me twice, choosing Richard and walking away from the things in herself that I most loved. It hurt. When someone you love moves on, if someone you love backs away, it leaves a hole. I have some gaping ones, and I've done some sorry things to fill them.

Soon after Pete and I were through, Sam started pressing for a reconciliation. I didn't regret the tryst, but I'd come out the other side seeing it for its emptiness. Trying again with Sam was looking good. But I was in a potholder mood and thought I'd have a little fun.

Sam hated I'd had the thing with Pete.

"A yoga instructor," he sneered. We were on the phone, but I could see his expression. "You couldn't do better? Do they let normal men be yoga instructors?"

"Sam," I said. "Your insecurity is showing. Forget about Pete. How about dinner? Tomorrow. Come to the house and we'll talk." I did intend to talk, but I also had in mind to torment him a little. Future generations will never call me Saint Antonia. I'm not above using every weapon I have.

Sam came over the next evening, and after we'd eaten I moved us into the living room with Irish coffee. Sam suddenly, peevishly, said, "So what kind of kinky things did he have the two of you doing?"

We were standing in front of the fireplace, the scene of that first romp with Pete. I turned and looked him dead-on. "How do you know I didn't do the initiating?"

That pierced, dead center. "Goddamn it, Toni." He threw his mug onto the mantel and pulled me to him. My coffee splashed everywhere. I laughed out loud, which provoked him even more. He grabbed my mug and plunked it next to his. Then he kissed me, the sort of kiss we hadn't ascended to in years. It was ferocious. I could hear our toes tingling. It was like discovering the Schwinn you rode as a kid stored in a corner of the garage. You hop onto the seat, and the full force of youth comes flooding back. Sam's hands fumbled at my clothes. His lips moved through my hair. "Don't tell me anything," he said, groaned, really. "I'd deserve it—but I don't want to know."

It was weird. I felt more footloose than I'd ever felt with him. I thought, *What the hell. He's my husband.* It wasn't like we'd be breaking any laws. I reached down and started unbuttoning his jeans.

Well. He froze. He pulled away with this awful look on his face. I tried to pull him back. "What's wrong?"

He turned away. "Maybe . . . this isn't such a good idea."

I spread my fingers lightly across the middle of his back. "Sam. Sam, please. What is it?"

"Oh, God. Toni."

The strain in his voice scared me. I pressed my fingers harder into his back. "Tell me." He shook his head, dropped his chin to his chest. I pressed my hands hard beneath his shoulder blades. "Sam. You can tell me."

His shoulders heaved. "Right. You're right—and you've got to know. It's . . . it's herpes," he said. "I've got herpes."

Herpes. The word reverberated in my ears and triggered a life review—of Sam's and my life together. I'd never envisioned this. Here I'd been moving toward trying again, had thought, in fact, I'd agree to it this evening, and now he was telling me this. I recoiled. I pulled my hands away. My mind was reeling, my tongue fell stone dead. I finally managed one earth-shatteringly intelligent word. "What?" Neither of us said anything for at least a minute. Then I managed a little sarcasm. "You've never heard of condoms?" I couldn't stop myself. To my knowledge, he hadn't been seeing anyone. "Who," I said, "were you sleeping with?"

He whirled around. "You're not exactly knitting potholders yourself, these days."

"Yeah? Well, maybe someone should have knit one for your dick."

The muscles in his jaw twitched. "This isn't what I need from you."

"I'm not the one running home knocked up."

"You think that's what this is? Christ. I've wanted to come home long before this. You're the one who's been dragging ass about it. I just got the damn virus."

"Great, Sam. You just got it. You haven't answered the question."

"A friend, of a friend. She said she was on the Pill. It was what she didn't say that got me. I'm not like you. I don't analyze every phrase and pick apart every situation."

I didn't say anything. I stared at the carpet.

He shook his head. "I feel—" Tears welled into his eyes. "Dirty." He started to cry. It was awful and harsh, like he didn't know how. "I thought about not telling you, about just . . . dropping out of sight. . . . But I didn't want to do that to you. I . . . I owe you better." His chest shuddered as he drew in a breath. "I don't know how to explain it. She was nice. I thought it was safe."

The famous last word . . .

What I knew about herpes might have filled a thimble. Once I got over the shock, I got analytical. My exposure to the subject had been limited to bad jokes. At work, we'd just put summer school to bed and were gearing up for fall. But for Sam's sake I couldn't go around discussing what he'd told me. Besides, herpes isn't the usual conversational fare in the faculty lounge:

"Morning, Toni. What's up?"

"Not much. Tried to jump Sam's ass last night, but he told me he's got the herp." A broad smile. "It nipped things right in the bud. What's new with you?"

No, this was something I needed to investigate on my own. Late in the day, I headed for the library. I found some articles, a medical encyclopedia, and a copy of *Our Bodies, Ourselves*. Just holding *Bodies* made me feel better. It was substantial and comforting. Rena had a copy when we were roommates, and we used to consult it like an oracle. I felt self-conscious, like the whole world knew what I was doing. I didn't go so far as to wear a scarf and dark glasses, but I came close. I sat discreetly in a corner of the stacks. The stats were that one in four adults has herpes. It blew me away. I'd never look at a crowd the same way. I started thinking about everyone I knew. Whose were the faces behind those clinical numbers?

I found out a couple needed to avoid sex during breakouts. But there was more bad news—there was a time before an actual lesion appeared when the virus could be passed. There was no way to know. The bottom line was, any woman in Sam's life would be at risk. The words of one infected woman were etched into my brain. "Herpes won't kill you, but it does a number on your sex life. And your head."

So. There was more to fear than fear itself.

I backed off from overtures toward Sam and got into the thing with Warren. But Sam wasn't deterred. After he'd come out of the closet, so to speak, he had nothing to lose. He stepped up his overtures toward me. "You haven't told me no yet. Have you?"

I lied. Well, a case of omission. There was a third night that changed my life. I was still rooming with Rena. She'd left on Friday for a shower and was coming back Sunday. The dorm was a morgue. The whole floor was gone—the only other person was a girl studying library science who was even sadder than me. I hung around the room all day Saturday, pretending to work. Walking back after dinner, I was filled suddenly with existential longing. I needed something, which I translated to someone. The thought went through my head, *I could do it, I could go out and find him.* I'd go somewhere and dance, have a couple screwdrivers and dance my tail off. I started running, like someone in love or gone nuts in a movie. At the room, I went helter-skelter through my clothes. I decided on my new hip-huggers and a midriff-baring top. It was the best I could do. I tried them on and thought, *I'm screwed. I don't even have good undies.* I looked at Rena's dresser. She had panties and bras that would kill. I didn't think, I didn't wonder if I should. I knew which drawer, and I opened it and pulled out the sweetest hot pink bra and matching bikini brief. I put them on, they even almost fit. I pulled the rest of my clothes back on and did final touches—hair in loose, sassy braids, dark green shadow on my eyes.

Walking in, the music was so loud I could feel it in my chest. It felt weird to take a table by myself, so I sat at the bar. I had a screwdriver. It was cool and it was good. Being in Rena's lingerie, I didn't feel like me. I liked it. I had another screwdriver, and then a guy asked me to dance—I did—and he bought me another one. I danced a few more dances and was back at my seat, on my fourth drink, when "Shame, Shame, Shame" ripped out of the speakers. By then, I didn't need an invitation. I twirled onto the floor. I didn't think my tail could do what my tail was doing. I was singing, and moving, and laughing—I felt so good. I closed my eyes, so I could watch the circles of light spinning in my head, and when I opened them, there was Richard. His eyes were inches from mine, and he was grinning. "Toni, Toni. What's got into you?"

"Screwdrivers."

We stood there. It could go either way.

Then and there, I decided I was going to have him, if I could. I started to dance, backing away, then forward, away, forward, and he mirrored me. We were on that floor the rest of the night, and then he walked me back to the dorm, and then to the room, and when I opened the door, he followed me in. I lit a candle—I don't know how, I was wobbly—but I managed to light it, and then . . . I couldn't believe it. It didn't click for him that I was in Rena's underthings. When he reached around, one-handed, and unsnapped the bra, I felt like I was with her and him and my head spun.

I don't know why he did it. Cold feet, maybe—the wedding was weeks away. He was drunk. He thought I was cute. Maybe he was taking pity, though I don't think so. On Monday, both of us cold sober, we met out on one of the walking paths on Picnic Point and did our mea culpas. We swore to go to the grave with it. We were still friends, only different. Richard and I love each other, but after that night, we knew, not like that. I was lucky not to get left with an unintended bonus.

I try to figure out why I did it. There were the screwdrivers. I was sweet on him—which he knew—and looking to poor mortals for something none could give. Hardest to admit, I was jealous of the two of them and hurt at the way she'd abandoned me. Having that night with him was, I suppose, a kind of payback. I felt wretched the next morning when Rena came back early and found me in bed, sick, sick. She took care of me all day, and the guilt nearly killed me.

I buy season tickets every year at Larkspur Theatre. Tonight, their new show opened. Sam showed up just as I was getting into my car to leave for the theatre and instigated another go-round. It wasn't a good time for it. I wasn't ready to see him. We ended up standing in the driveway, arguing. It was dark and it was cold. The wind was getting nasty. Finally, I snapped at him, "Friggin' get off my back."

"All right," he said. "You called it."

He sounded like maybe he meant it. I stepped into my car and threw it in reverse. Sam had gotten left leaning against his hood, and as I drove away, I could feel his eyes boring holes into my taillights. Fortunately, I knew the ushers, and they let me in even though the show had started. The play they're doing now is confusing by design to keep the audience off-balance. I was glad I'd read it before I'd come. Otherwise, I couldn't possibly have figured out what was afoot, and the humor would have been lost on me.

Claire Collier was in the cast. She goes to Pelican. Her performances are always strong, but tonight she was meteoric. She burned and burned and never gave out, she projected this unworldly energy. Hers wasn't a major role, but I found my eyes following her.

Claire married a colleague of mine, let's see, when she was about ten. Sounds catty, but it's not that much of an exaggeration. Paul Collier is one of my more likable colleagues. He's sharp but doesn't need to be the most brilliant voice in the

room. He went through a bad divorce my first year here. He'd
been married to the first Mrs. Collier about six months, when
he discovered his new wife's car parked overnight in another
man's driveway. Unfortunately, the man was his department
chair, who at midyear accepted a job at a research institute and
took along Paul's wife.

The rumor raged across campus like an inferno. The
phones were so hot, every department on campus smelled of
smoke. We hadn't had something that sizzling to receive and
pass on since the first week of the semester, when word broke
that the dean of humanities had taken up with the new mayor.
The dean had just observed her twenty-fifth anniversary, replete
with white tent and orchestra. After the debacle of his wife's conduct, Paul disappeared from public view for a while but eventually resurfaced, not obviously the worse for wear. Everyone was
glad to see it. But when he got involved with Claire, it was awkward. She was so young, not to mention in some of our classes.

He and I were on the curriculum committee then, which,
like most committees, met late in the day. The first meeting after
I'd heard he was seeing Claire, after we adjourned he showed
up at my office. My briefcase was on the chair next to my desk,
coat and lunch bucket stacked on top. It was obvious I was on
my way out.

"Got a minute?" he said.

"Of course."

I cleared off the chair, and he flopped onto it and crossed
the ankle of one leg over the knee of the other. "So," he said,
"there's this big animal in the room, and no one brings it up. It's
trumpeting, snorting chaff, you can't see across the table for all
the crap it's blown in the air, but no one says, 'What the hell?'
I thought you were going to, when you first came in. Just before
the bell, I might add, as usual. I thought you were upfront
enough to say something. You gave me that look, Toni's winding

up, and I thought, 'She's going to, she's going to say it. Leave it to Toni, thank God.'" He studied me, not a hard look, but a wondering one. "But you didn't."

"Well." I couldn't think. What would be best to say? "It's just . . . it's . . . for crying out loud, Paul, I'd think you'd be the one. It's your place. What do we know about it? 'Collier's seeing a student, what's he thinking?' What are we supposed to say?"

"Maybe 'Say, Paul, I hear you're seeing someone.'" He extended one hand toward me, palm up, giving me my entrée.

"Say," I said, "I hear . . . you're seeing someone."

"I am. She's fresh, alive. I guess I don't have to say it's complicated. . . . I'm the most content I've ever been." The look on his face made me envious. I hadn't been there in a long time.

"Hey," I said. "I'm happy for you. Really, with all you've been through."

"Forget all that." He extended his hand again, offering a shake. I took it, and he said, "Thanks." He stood and moved to the door, but instead of leaving, he stopped and leaned against the jamb. "I'm not being rash, Toni. I thought hard about it. Claire's not in my department, she won't be taking my classes. I've had my little talk with the dean, at my request, not hers. It matters to me, what some of you think."

After he'd gone, I felt bad I hadn't said something before I'd left the meeting. Sometimes, in fraught situations with people I don't know well, my brain seizes and for lack of words I abdicate. It's a poor strategy. Words withheld, when words are called for, are as bad as hard words spoken. Paul went on to marry Claire, but that marriage, too, ended up under the skids.

I don't know Claire. She's only recently showed up at the church, and Sam and I didn't move in the same circles as she and Paul. We'd see them at faculty things, and once or twice spent the evening at the same dinner party, where Claire barely said a word. She was such a child. I've often wondered. How does someone that untried get through something like divorce?

During intermission, the big news was that Marcus Talbot was dead. A coronary, someone said. Marcus and his wife, Lucy, are mucky-mucks around town. Marcus is—was—the type you never get to know, no matter how long you've known him. One weekend, Sam and I drove down to the Hotel Fullerton to hear a jazz band, and who did we see but Marcus, squiring a petite woman in a sequined dress. She looked all of thirty. He saw us, but when our eyes met, he looked right through us. Then the following Sunday at church, he was his usual affable, ineffable self.

Sam and I never breathed a word. But after church that day on our way to brunch, we speculated. Actually, Sam started it. He was driving, and I was reading the paper. As he pulled into the parking spot at the restaurant, he gave the paper a whack. I hated when he did things like that. He said, "What do you think? What's going on in that house on the hill?"

"I don't know. You tell me." I folded the paper on my lap.

"Come on, Toni. Play with me. Who was the woman? Who was he with?"

"Who knows? Family friend? Relative? Inamorata?" I opened my door and stepped out.

"Inamorata?" Sam exclaimed from the driver's seat. He hopped out and caught up. "Jesus, Toni. Where do you come up with those words?" He slipped an arm around my waist. "Baby, I'm guessing love nests on the side—for both Marcus and Lucy."

"Sam. Someone will hear you."

"No one's around. Lucy's a babe, and on the prowl. I'm telling you, it's booty on every side."

After I left the theatre, I stopped at my office and didn't get home until after eleven. I'd been thinking all evening about Claire Collier—how ethereal she'd looked, I was still reacting on a visceral level—and also about the Talbots. I guess whenever someone dies, you feel a tug on the big web. Seeing Lucy and Marcus together, a person might not call them the apple of each other's eye, but they also wouldn't guess there were serious problems. After what Sam and I had seen, though, down at the Fullerton, I figured Lucy was jumping in the air and clicking her heels about now.

I'd been thinking hardest about my own quandary. If I took Sam back, we'd face some large new problems on top of what we'd already had. I kept asking myself, would it be too much? Could we even do it? That is, if he was still talking to me after the scene in the driveway.

I scuttled across the yard, clutching my coat against the wind. There was sleet in the forecast, and the front was moving in. The chimes on the patio were rippling, calling like a lost sea bird. I was almost to the door before I heard the phone ringing. Damn. I'd forgotten to turn on the machine. I hate that feeling. It might be someone you really want to talk to, and you've no idea if it's the first ring or the twentieth. Whoever's on the line could hang up at any second. What if it was Sam? My first impulse was, *Screw it, don't answer.* But a second later, an image flashed through my mind—me, balanced on a high wire, just me—and I nearly stripped the lock getting the key in and out. I dropped my briefcase and lunged for the desk to grab the phone.

It was Rena. "Hi," she said.

"Rena." I had this vague sense of disappointment that must have come through on her end.

"You okay?" she said. "You sound a little down."

"Just tired."

"Ah. I'm tired myself. I won't keep you." She sounded like she'd had one of those days, too. "I've been trying to get you for an hour—even tried your office. Where have you been?"

"The play. Well, the office, too, but only for a few minutes."

"Uh-huh . . . the play. How was it?"

"Good, really good. You should have been there. Claire Collier was a Roman candle—the woman was all over the stage. It was like she was on something. She could have played the *Midsummer Night's* fairies all by herself."

"We've . . . we've been talking about seeing it. I suppose we will. You heard about Marcus?"

"Yeah, at the show."

"Richard was with Lucy all evening. She found Marcus in the yard. He'd been splitting kindling, was already gone when she got there. Bugs and Naomi are with her—they'll spend the night." She sighed. "I'm glad she's not there alone."

"Me, too. I guess sometimes we get things right." I couldn't help but wonder. "Did Richard say . . . how Lucy's taking it?"

"Hard. He said—" Her voice caught. "He said he hated to leave her and come home."

"No kidding?" Lucy's famous for riding herd on the church staff, so for Richard to stay with her a moment beyond what was necessary was something to contemplate.

We fell silent.

"So," Rena said, "why I'm calling. Joey flies in tomorrow, and Lawrence will join him on Monday. He has a show this weekend at some big gallery, and he'll take care of boarding their cats. The funeral will be on Tuesday. Can you help with the luncheon? Make some bars? Maybe help serve?"

I told her I would, anything she needed, and she said, "Thanks, that'll . . . it's a help. I'm running on half my cylinders. I've been . . . yeah." She finished the thought only in her own head. "I'm wiped. Call you tomorrow?"

"Sure. Or I can call you."

"No. I'll call. I . . . we . . . we need to talk." For a few beats my heart tripped over itself. Oh, God. Had Richard told her? I knew he might, someday, he might have to, and we'd be living with the consequences, but . . . we live with consequences, either way. It wasn't that, though. At least, I don't think. Rena hesitated, I heard her breath suck in, and then she said, "Toni. Richard didn't—he didn't want to come home."

Before I could say, "What?" the receiver hummed. She'd hung up.

I sat there, thinking about what Rena had said, about Richard. Something profound had happened—something had opened between us. She hadn't said anything that real in years. A train whistle started to blow. Trains are so much a part of the landscape here we almost don't hear them. But this one, I heard. It was a long, mournful howl. I propped my elbows on the desk, clasped my hands, and listened. I got lost in it. It came into my head the train was here for Marcus.

Then it was gone. The silence descended again, windswept, punctuated by chimes. I was completely alone in it, I was completely at home—and just like that, I knew. I knew what I wanted. No trauma, no drama. Who would know joy was so small? My hands flew up for a moment to my face, then I grabbed the highlighter and marked the day on the calendar. It was as if an angelic messenger opened a door and sang out, "Interior-gram for Antonia Sprague-Heller." Only this time the angel wasn't a janitor. It was a businesswoman, named Lucy—a woman who would not imagine herself angelic, who had unknowingly sent her grief.

I wanted Sam. He was where I needed to be. I wanted the years back, wanted the friend. I wanted that flimsy piece of paper. I wanted the ease of us, the maddening difficulty. I wanted the highs, the lows, the boredom even. We'd both sown some wild oats in our middle-aged dreams. We'd both taken risks. If I caught something from him—herpes, or worse—there'd be a poetic justice in it.

I lifted the phone and punched the numbers in. By magic, and fiber optics, the energy I pressed into the pad raced along the line. The world was holding its breath. The enormity of the decision and the moment increased with every ring. *Ri-i-ing, ri-i-ing, ri-i-ing, ri-i-ing, ri-i-ing*— The man was something else. He refused to buy an answering machine. Just as I was about to hang up, in absolute frustration, he picked up.

"Hello." His dear voice was heavy with sleep.

"Hi. It's me."

Light

The town was moving toward sleep. Darkened storefront
windows shimmied as the wind touched and moved past
them. The main street was quiet now—vehicles moved with long
spaces between them. A group of revelers stood at the pedes-
trian light on the corner by the convenience store, where the
lights were still on. The signal light was against them. There was
a break in the traffic, and one reveler stepped out, moved to
cross against the light. Another drew him back. The group
laughed and argued happily about traffic laws, huddling for
warmth. The light changed, and they crossed.

In a residential part of town, the wind knocked over a spindly
geranium on the porch of a house. Inside, a woman was on the
phone—so engrossed in what she was saying, she didn't hear the
plant fall. The neighbor next door, coming home from a frater-
nal organization, heard the chimes in her yard and saw her
through the window. *Good,* he thought. *She's home.* He would
tell his wife, and they would go to bed. They were retired but
used their time. Their neighbor lived alone, her husband moved
out, months now. They checked for her lights every night.

The train was outside the reach of the ear, moving through
wind-driven countryside to the next pool of light. Out on the
lake, the lights of a ship sailed past. It was a big ship, beyond
the harbor.

Both would be back.

On the bluff above town, the wind vane on the roof of the church hummed steadily, with rapid starts and stops. In the blowing light from the parking lot, its wings seemed to have lifted now and were flapping, some sort of joy.

High, high above, like a single bead, the pelican flew.

Acknowledgments

Many have contributed to this book. My sister Diane Salli Crang, our family librarian, read and reread the manuscript, her hip and lucid comments and questions shining a light. My husband, Bruce Eastman, has supported me in every way, especially by lending his exacting poet's eye, and my colleague Brandy Lindquist brought a scholar's eye and knocked me off my coffee shop chair with her close attention to the manuscript.

I'm deeply grateful for the support and encouragement of arts organizations. This novel was made possible in part by a grant provided by the Five Wings Arts Council, with funds from the McKnight Foundation supplemented with Legacy funds. That grant supported my attending a novel-writing conference at the Loft Literary Center that proved a turning point as I worked on the book. I am further indebted to the Loft for its awarding me a Mentor Series Award. I was given a year to write, along with a talented and generous group of other young writers, to discuss our work, and to learn together from established poets and prose writers. Lastly, I am grateful to the Great Plains Theatre Conference, where I spent a week as a participating playwright and learned volumes about the art of a story.

A Notion of Pelicans could not exist, of course, without those who saw it into print. My agent and publicist, Krista Rolfzen Soukup, is a force, both knowledgeable and dynamic. The people at North Star Press, Anne Rasset, Corinne Dwyer, and Curtis Weinrich, have brought equal parts savvy and love to the book, and Chip Borkenhagen of Riverplace dreamed into being the ethereal cover art and also designed the novel's cover and family tree. George Marsolek and the Central Lakes College Theatre Department lent their stage and lighting expertise for a photo shoot, and John Erickson, who wielded the camera, brought a unique artistry to the creation of my author portrait. Finally, Corey Kretsinger developed my website, creating around the novel an online world and tutoring me in its mysteries.